THE WRITE CHOICE

JAMI ROGERS

For Kristin Songe and Zara Keyser
"Is 19 inches too big?"

Cover design © Hang Le byhangle.com

Elements Cover Design by Erika Plum Designs

Editor: Julie Sturgeon, CEO Editor, ceoeditor.com

Proofreading: Owl Eyes Proof and Edits, www.owleyesproofsedits.com

Visit my website: www.authorjamirogers.com

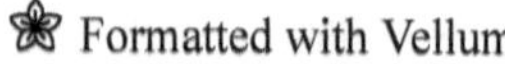 Formatted with Vellum

THE WRITE CHOICE

JAMI ROGERS

CHAPTER ONE
BECK

I'm surprisingly good at sneaking around. A lot better than I would have assumed, honestly. I can't say it's an excellent quality or even one I'm happy to have acquired, but it does come in handy.

I close the door to my new home office and let out a breath. Having my friends over for dinner and hanging out in my backyard was exactly what I needed. I've never been more proud of myself than I am right now. Not only is my release from last week still in the top three of *Lovers Magazine's* best-sellers list, but I'm officially a homeowner. It only took me thirty years for the second part, but this house is perfect. Not just for me, but for the future wife and kids I plan to have.

Yep, that's me. Beck Robertson. Hopeless romantic—or hopeful if you want to get technical—who just so happens to write romance novels. They're damn good too. Obviously, since I'm on a bestsellers list. Okay, so I'm a little cocky too. I can't help it. Confidence has never been something I struggle with. When I was a kid, my grandpa told me that I have to live the life I want. *Don't get stuck in a life you wish you were living.* I know, it's a little wonky. Grandpa loved his whiskey, but the point is, I wanted to live a life of confidence, control, and success from a young age, and now, being an adult, well, I'm successfully living the life I've always dreamed of having.

Minus the reason I snuck into my office.

I scan the white wall with floor-to-ceiling bookshelves behind my desk. My gaze glides over how much more work I need to do—nothing has been unpacked to fill them yet—and then to my desk. It's a mess, too. In fact, the room isn't even close to being organized. The desk is together and there's a chair and my computer is open and ready to use. Technically, that's all I need at this point.

Oh, and a damn good idea for my next book.

Fuck. I'm drawing a blank.

Without an idea of what my next book is going to be about, I can't even focus on having a couple hours of fun with my friends. Now, I know I'm more than just a romance writer, but hell, this is one of my favorite parts of my life and I'm… stuck.

I drop into my seat and pull my phone from my pocket. Doug, my agent, has been texting me for two days now, but it's the latest message that stresses me out the most.

Doug: These chapters are shit, Beck. Do you still want this double book and movie deal or not? Give me something better. Again.

. . .

Fucking hell.

Again.

Again!

And yeah, I want that movie deal. What author would pass that up?

I'd like to type back a snarky reply, tell him he shouldn't talk to me like that. I'm his client. I deserve respect, but considering we go back to our college years and have competed against each other chugging a beer bong upside down, praying the liquid doesn't come gushing from our noses at numerous frat parties before our careers started, I know he's just being honest, and in the end, his ability to tell me how it is will help me in the long run.

Plus, he's not wrong. The chapters he's referring to are the fourth set of beginning chapters for a new book. They've all sucked. I knew it before I even sent them, but hey, something is better than nothing, right?

Not to mention, writers are known to be hard on themselves. Something I might think is boring as hell might be gold in the eyes of another.

I open a Word document and just stare at the screen, the sound of laughter outside my window pulling my attention. Now isn't the time to start a new book. I have guests. Then again, considering all my friends are romance writers themselves, they'd understand. Hero was just in this spot a little over a year ago. Struggling to write because of an outside event that wouldn't let his mind calm down enough to focus on his creativity. For him, it was a bad review.

Me?

That's not my problem.

Simon would tell me to relax and take a few days off to

let my mind rest. Tobias would tell me to step out of my lane. That's a hard no for me. He's the only romance writer I know who can write whatever he wants whenever he wants and get away with it. Then there's Graham, and while he would have sound advice, our writing couldn't be more different. I'm all about the slow burn, no clothes, saucy shit, and he's… milk and cookies with an arm around her shoulders while they watch the Hallmark Channel. Which means our approach to what helps the process is different. Zane would be down to go on a run with me. He never seems to struggle with plot issues, and he's great at helping me fix mine.

So, yeah, I have a lot of options, but truth be told, they'd all ask what happened to cause this disruption in my writing life, and I'm not ready to talk about it with any of them. I'm not even sure what the hell is going on myself.

I snap my MacBook closed and head out of my office.

Staring at nothing isn't going to help me.

I jog up my basement steps and am just about to open one of my French patio doors just off the dining room when Calla, Simon's younger sister and the biggest pain in my ass, grabs my wrist and pulls me down the upstairs hallway. It takes everything I have not to roll my eyes. I swear, I don't know what it is, but this woman… hell, she deflates my maturity by twenty years.

"What?" I ask and pinch the spot between my eyes. Between her and my book problems, I need to find some advice.

She peeks over my shoulder in the direction we just came from and then pins me with a glare.

As soon as my eyes lock on hers, my heartbeat picks up

pace and the memory of the last time we were alone takes over.

I swallow, a grin tugging at my lips. The gesture only annoys her more.

"Why haven't you answered my texts or phone calls?"

I lick my lips and nod.

Now, I know what you're thinking. We hooked up, and she got attached, and I just ghosted her because she's my best friend's sister and the rules of life basically forbid it.

Nope. Not even close.

"Beck, answer me before someone finds us."

I reach for her, but she swats my hand away.

"What do you want me to say, Calla? I haven't answered your texts or calls for a reason."

Her green eyes shine like a rare emerald against her bright blonde hair pulled on top of her head into a messy bun. I wouldn't mind letting it down and giving it a good tug with her on her knees in front of me. But there is no way in hell I'd tell her that.

She stomps her foot. "It's a stupid reason and one I don't agree with."

I shrug. "Give me a different offer and maybe we can talk."

I move to pass her, but she stops me with a hand on my chest.

"I have only one offer, Beck, and it isn't changing."

Heat pricks at every part of my body as I grind my teeth.

"Neither is mine."

She holds her gaze steady with mine. I rest one hand flat on the wall next to her head and lean in so close, I can feel her breath brush over my cheek.

My lips part to speak, but she pushes me back. The anger in her eyes deflates.

"Please, Beck. Please. I'll do anything you want."

My brow peaks, and she rolls her eyes. "Don't be dirty. Seriously, you come off as the most innocent of the group, but deep down, I think you're the worst."

"You used to like that once upon a time."

She slaps my shoulder. "Be an adult about this."

"I am," I chuckle.

"You are not."

"Beck! Where are you?" Simon's voice carries through my main floor, and Calla's eyes go wide. "I spilled my beer all over your brand-new patio table, and I need more paper towels."

"Looks like I have to go."

"Beck," Calla says in a sharp whisper that stops me in my tracks. "You can fight this as much as you want, but at the end of the day, I still want a divorce."

The last word is like a knife through my heart.

"I know you do," I say and bow my head before leaving.

The thing is, I don't.

CHAPTER TWO
BECK - VEGAS

I can't stop staring at Hero and Nora.

I want what they have.

Maybe I'm too desperate to find true love. Maybe my books turn women away because they think that's what I want. Maybe I hold my standards too high. I mean hell, for as far back as my family can remember, not a single Robertson has ever been divorced. It's not in our genes. So yeah, my standards are high. The pressure is high. I get one chance. I can't mess it up.

Maybe I'm overthinking it.

"You want to go grab a beer or two before we call it a night?" Zane asks, his attention on his phone. Probably texting his "non-girlfriend" Willa.

Riiight. They aren't dating, my ass. Those two are as committed as the soon-to-be newlyweds sharing a seat across from me.

Fuck.

Everyone around me is happily settling down, and then there's me. Happy as hell for them but envious as fuck.

Wanting to be in love isn't a crime. It doesn't make me pathetic or sappy or whatever you want to call it just because I want that and don't have it.

It makes me human.

Fucking hell, I need a drink or two.

"Yeah. Let's go."

I stand just as Hero says, "We're going to call it a night, but let's still plan to meet poolside tomorrow, yeah?"

"Oh, it's so cute how you all keep your traditions on tour. Poolside on your day off."

Hero pinches Nora's side, and she laughs before he kisses her.

Shots. I need shots too.

Zane and I say goodbye to the lovebirds and head out of the restaurant and down the Strip. Signings in Vegas are a lot of work, but they're some of my favorites. Normally, we don't stay on the Strip, but we changed it up this year. It also helped that Simon brought his son because his summer babysitter quit at the last minute. He thought the Strip would be more fun for him. Roller coasters and whatnot. So far, his favorite has been M&M's World.

"Hey, wait up!" a female voice says. It's one I know all too well.

Simon's sister. Calla.

"Calla, are you heading out on the town?" Zane jokes with her.

"Not exactly. Just a drink or two. I ran into Nora in the elevator, and she said you two just left, so I thought I'd catch up."

Her eyes lock on mine, and I can tell she's just itching to say something snarky.

I beat her to it.

"What, no one needed an escort tonight?"

I skim her outfit.

I know what I said. I know it was shitty. But fuck, what was I supposed to say? Wear that dress again and I'll tear it off myself?

Nope. Can't say that.

So, be a dick it is.

"You know what? I'm not even going to respond to that. I'm in a great mood today, thank you very much."

"Oh yeah, why?" Zane asks as we all fall into step.

"I got a job. I'm officially moving to Wind Valley at the end of the summer."

I turn to her, ready to reply, but catch the stern look on Zane's face first, then the sharp shake of his head.

"Congratulations, Calla. I bet Simon is thrilled," he says to her.

"He is. My parents, not so much."

"Why not? You're an adult. You're twenty-nine now, right?"

"Yes, and I don't know how to explain it. I'm... oh! I'm a pantser, if you want to use writer's terms."

"Makes sense, then."

I listen as the two of them carry on conversation for about another block before Zane stops abruptly.

"Umm," he says and flashes his phone to us to show that Willa is calling. "I'm gonna take a rain check."

"No!" Calla cries out while I try not to grind my teeth.

"Think you two can survive?" he asks, backing up.

"Of course." Calla smiles.

I'm still glaring at him.

"Good. Night!"

We both stand there until Zane is out of sight.

"Night, Beck."

Calla turns on her heel.

"Where are you going?"

"To get a drink. Without you. I don't want you to ruin my mood."

"You're not getting a drink alone."

"Yes, I am."

"The hell you are. Simon would kill me if he knew I let you go out alone in Vegas wearing a dress like that."

"What kind of dress am I wearing?" She spins and I bump into her.

"No way. I'm not playing this. As your brother's longest best friend, I've known you since you were ten, and I know your games. You know you're fucking sexy, Calla. I'm not letting you go out alone."

"Wrong. And compliment or not, I don't want you to come."

"You don't get a choice." I continue to follow her as she heads into the MGM, my eyes fighting to look anywhere but at her supple ass.

I'm not a perv. She's just too damn good to look away from. Has been since we were in high school, but like every other thought I have for Calla, I'm not about to tell her that.

"Wrong again. Goodbye, Beck."

I pause as she heads into one of the bars. As soon as she takes a seat, I walk in and take the one next to her. I twist my stool so we aren't stuck face-to-face, breathing on each other, but whether she likes it or not, I'm going where she goes.

She groans, loudly, and the bartender looks back and forth between us before deciding to ignore whatever thought he had.

"Drinks?" he asks.

"Moscow mule, please," Calla says without thinking twice.

"Just a beer for me, thank you."

"Brand?"

"Your favorite on draft." I couldn't care less what I'm drinking right now. I'll most likely be nursing it so that I can keep an eye on Calla.

"And a shot of vodka, please," Calla adds.

"Yeah, good idea. Get shitfaced and wander around Vegas."

"Oh, are you jealous I'm going to have fun tonight and you aren't?"

"Hardly."

"God, you're boring."

I roll my eyes.

"If she takes a shot, I take a shot," I tell the bartender.

Fuck, this is going to be a long night.

CHAPTER THREE
CALLA

"Put a finger up if you married your mortal enemy one night in Vegas and now, he won't give you a divorce." I fake glance around my bathroom as if there are others getting ready with me. "No one else, no? Just me."

Freaking fantastic. And now I'm talking to myself.

I finish applying my mascara then turn off the lights to the bathroom, my room, and the basement before heading up to my brother's kitchen.

"Good morning," I say, spotting said brother and my nephew, Grey, sitting at the table eating breakfast. "Ooh, that looks yummy."

I scuff up the hair on Grey's head and grab a plate.

"Are you nervous about today?" Simon asks.

"What's happening today?" Grey asks him.

"I'm starting a new job," I answer for my brother.

"That makes you nervous?"

I shake my head. "Nope."

I catch my brother's eye roll as soon as I drop to my seat at the table.

"What?"

"Nothing." He shakes his head and stuffs his mouth with scrambled eggs.

"Say it."

He glances at Grey, who, the spitting image of his father, catches on quickly and shakes his head, too. "I'm done anyway."

"Brush your teeth and make your bed. I'll be up in ten minutes to check before we leave for school."

"Fine," Grey sighs, heading down the hall to his room.

As soon as we hear his bedroom door shut, Simon leans forward, elbows on the table.

"Think you'll keep this job longer than a month?" he asks.

"I plan to."

"Good."

"And if not, I'll just find a new one."

"Calla," Simons groans. "You're almost thirty. You should have a career by now."

"Whoa, no. Stop right there. I already had this lecture from Mom and Dad before I left last week, alright. I don't need it from you, either."

"We just—"

"No. Simon, it's normal for people to be almost thirty and not have things figured out."

"Yeah, but most people want to have things figured out, and I don't think you do."

I shrug. "So what? I don't like to be tied down to anything. Maybe my life plan is to keep things exciting by changing things up every couple of months."

Instead of answering, he sighs and grabs his plate and mine, now that it's empty, too.

"I just worry about you. That's all."

"Okay, but don't. I'm fine."

He nods. "Good luck today."

"Thanks." I head back down the stairs to brush my teeth.

I quickly finish getting ready and drive the short distance to work.

I pull into the parking lot of my new job. Am I thrilled for this job? No. It's not anything I particularly want to be doing, but my brother was kind enough to offer his basement until I found a place to live. So I sort of just took the first thing offered to me.

I'm a billing clerk.

Whoo, fun. Stuck behind a desk for eight hours a day looking at numbers. Yuck.

But three months ago, I made the choice to move from Melody, Wyoming, my hometown, to Wind Valley, Wyoming. I'm not running from anything, but I just keep thinking something is missing. I don't know what it is, but I hadn't found it living in Melody, so I was desperate to leave. To get a fresh start. To start making better choices.

Better choices. Ha.

Well, we all know how great that's been working for me. I can basically hear my mother now.

Calla, you make too many rash decisions.

Calla, you didn't think this through, did you?

Calla, what were you thinking?

So, yeah, when I said I was moving, I also lied and said I had a job. Then this came up.

I'm not sure what I'm getting myself into. I don't even

know what a billing clerk does. Billing, I guess. It's insane how easy it is to lie on a résumé and get away with it.

My phone vibrates in my purse. I dig it out as if it's ticking bomb, only to see a text wishing me good luck from my friends Nora and Greer.

I was hoping it was a text from Beck, finally caving and agreeing to free me from my latest bad choice.

God, that man infuriates me.

I glance at the building in front of me and close my eyes.

Nothing against the job, but I have more pressing issues to deal with today. I need to hunt Beck down and get him to agree to a divorce.

Vegas was a mistake, and we need to erase it.

Sadly, as it turns out, I married the most stubborn man in Wyoming.

I fix my hair and straighten my navy pencil skirt before heading inside.

The entire room is in chaos before the door has even closed behind me.

People are rushing around, and someone is speed walking past me, crying and carrying a box. More people follow with boxes of their own but fewer tears. Others, without boxes, look like a deer in the headlights.

Well, this should be fun.

Suddenly, someone is yelling, and I'm not sure where to look first: toward the noise, the group of criers, or the receptionist desk.

"Can I help you?"

I snap my attention to the man behind the reception desk. Thank god someone made that choice for me. He's got dark hair combed over to the left, thin glasses, and a white button-down shirt. There's a crease between his brows—he isn't too excited to help me.

"Yes, I'm Calla Stone. I'm here for my first day as a billing clerk." I grab the stack of magazines to my left and straighten them, and then I swap the hand sanitizer and the Kleenex. There, those placements look much better.

The guy's face wrinkles instantly, and he closes his eyes.

"No one called you?"

"Called me for what?"

"The billing department was absorbed as of closing time yesterday."

"Absorbed?"

He nods. "Absorbed."

Now, I have a hunch that means I don't have a job, but for clarification purposes, I need him to say the actual words.

"So that means…"

"There is no job for you here," he says with the most sincerity I think he can muster.

"Ah."

"Sorry."

I beam. This is fine. I have time to gather myself and find a new job. Luckily for me, I've already planned to stay with my brother a few months and won't have to pay rent or bills aside from groceries for myself. I have money saved up. In Melody, I worked for my parents at their bookstore, and they paid me better than they should have.

Still…

This is why you don't make rash choices, Calla. Do your research next time.

My mother's voice is on autopilot in my mind.

Maybe I just won't tell my mom about this. Or my

brother. Or my dad. In fact, I'll just keep it to myself until I have another job lined up.

I give a pathetic wave and head out the door.

Yep, this is me. Calla Stone. Twenty-nine-year-old female with no degree and no job, can't make the right choice to save my life and living with my older brother and nephew in their basement.

Thriving, huh?

I like to pretend that not having my shit together doesn't faze me, but it does. Oh, it does. But my family has spent too many years coddling me. At some point, I decided to just pretend that everything is okay all the time. This is no different.

But crap, what happens if I never figure things out? Is that the thing missing from my life?

Oh God. Does this mean I'll be one of those people who works till the day she dies because she wasn't able to hold a job long enough to build a retirement?

I let out a few quick breaths.

Okay, that's not going to happen. I'm ambitious. I will find a new job.

I'm going to find myself the best job, and I'm going to make it last.

For once, I will make something last.

CHAPTER FOUR

BECK

Texts from my agent started at sunrise today, and I've been dwelling on one message in particular:

Is there anything in your real life that could spark a good book?

Getting married in Vegas to a woman who despises you could make a pretty good story. And yet, since I'm actually living it, I can't seem to think of how that story would play out. I have a good suspicion that it's because I have no idea what I'm doing. Hence, what would I make a character do in this situation?

The hero could trick her into staying married to help him achieve something. Or the heroine could ask him to keep up the illusion of a happy couple to make an ex jealous.

Those ideas have been done before, but they work. Over and over.

Still, the fact that my intention to stay married is nothing close to either option makes it weird for me to write about it.

Then again, my best ideas come from just getting words

on paper, and hell, maybe if I started writing this book, I'd be able to figure out what to do about Calla.

I can't just explain to her why I think we should stay married. She'll tell me tough luck and shove divorce papers in my face. I need another idea. I have to show her why being married to me is the right choice.

I jog down the stairs to my basement and head for my office, where I open the document for the last book I'd submitted to Doug and delete the words that I won't be needing for a book I won't be writing. I used to cringe at the idea of deleting unused words, but over time, the clean slate of just starting over has mentally worked the best for me.

I get in about three pages before my phone starts to ring.

It's Simon.

Our weekly writers' meeting is at his house this week, so I bet he's calling to change plans.

"Hey, Simon, what's up?"

"Can you come over?" His words are rushed.

"Right now?"

"Yes. Now."

"Is everything okay?" I ask, standing and grabbing my keys.

"Grey and I are fine, if that's what you mean."

"Okay, good."

"I'll fill you in when you get here."

"I'm on my way."

Fifteen minutes later, I'm standing on Simon's stairs, looking at about ten big fans in his basement.

"Calla is going to be furious when she gets here."

I let out a small chuckle. Yeah, for once, I might not be at the top of her shit list. Although, to Simon's credit, it's not his fault his basement flooded.

"Did you at least give her a heads-up?" If I'm lucky, I won't be here to witness her reaction.

"Yeah, I called her. She said she would head over right away, but it's her first day at a new job. I should have waited."

"Wait, so she's headed here now?"

He nods.

"Well, that's my cue." I clasp a hand on his shoulder and turn to head back up his steps.

"Wait. I need a favor."

I have a good feeling I know where he's going with this, and our decades-long friendship is the only reason I'm not already in my SUV.

I slowly turn and cock one brow.

"What?"

"Have an open mind, alright?"

"Simon!" Calla's voice rings through the house as she jogs down the steps. "Is every—what's he doing here?"

"Well," he starts, and she pauses before she reaches the step I'm on. "I need you to have an open mind."

"Simon," she snaps. "What did you do?"

His hands go up in surrender. "I said have an open mind, didn't I?"

Then his gaze bounces back and forth between me and Calla.

"No."

"No, no, no."

"I'm not living with him."

"Dude, you have really lost your mind, haven't you? Do you need a vacation?" I ask him.

Simon's head drops back as he takes a breath.

"Just hear me out. You're both being overly dramatic," he says.

Calla rolls her eyes, and I shake my head.

"Unbelievable," she groans and retreats up the steps.

Doug's words from our earlier conversation play in my head as Simon relentlessly goes on about his sister needing a place to stay.

This is about as good as it gets, Doug.

Sure, okay, my life has good book qualities, but I don't want to write a good book. I want a sinfully enjoyable book that people fall in love with. This might be the plot twist I need to clear my mind. I'll put it on paper to sort it out. But that's all.

"Come on, Beck, help me out," Simon says before I get the chance to make my own exit. "I could put her up in a hotel, but that could be a couple hundred bucks a night and this could take weeks to be fixed."

"Simon, your sister hates me."

Even more so now that I won't give her what she wants.

He cringes. "She doesn't exactly hate you. You two are just vastly different."

He jogs up the steps and out to the back patio where Grey is playing on a handheld PS2, his wireless earbuds in.

"Your family owns a bookstore, and I write books." I hold my hands up. "Not that much different."

"Well then, this will give you plenty of time to figure out what's wrong."

I hesitate.

Now, look, previous interactions and thoughts of Calla

have left me conflicted. Do I want to stay married to her? Yes. Do I want to live with her? No.

It makes zero sense to me too.

All I know is that marriage in my family is sacred. I refuse to be the first on both sides of my family tree to get a divorce. Why? It's pretty much an unspoken rule in my family that once you make that commitment, you don't break it. Ever. You do everything in your power to keep it. I've had the best role models to show me how to do this, and failing to show them how much I learned from them after all these years would be humiliating. That and divorcé isn't something I care to add to my reputation or bio as a romance writer.

Aside from those two fun facts about my life, when two people make a choice to bond their lives forever, drunk or not, there's a reason, right? I want to find out what that reason is. It's probably going to kill me or drive me so insane we split anyway, but I won't know unless I try.

Now, I don't exactly have a plan, but moving in together is not the way to do that.

"Between you, Tobias, and Graham, she'll be the most comfortable with you because she has known you the longest and is around you the most. Trust me. Please help me out." He puts his hands together in prayer form. "I'll get on my knees."

As much as I'd love to see him grovel over this, I'm not a dick.

Yes, this is a bad, *bad* idea, but also, this is my best friend and his sister, and they need my help.

"Fine."

"Yes! One month, tops."

"One month? You just said weeks."

"Well, yeah, but if she finds a house, what's the point of moving from your place or mine to a new one?"

I can't even form an answer. I just shake my head.

"I guess she'll have the basement to herself, aside from when I'm in my office. You owe me."

"Yes!" he says with a snap of his fingers.

"Calla, he's in," Simon shouts into the house from where we sit on his patio. "You'll have your own room at his place."

"I'm not living with him!" she snaps.

Again, I toss up my hands.

"What's wrong with Beck?" Simon asks her. "Honestly, give me a real answer." I'm about to suggest that he shouldn't argue with her, but I'm curious about this answer myself. How far into the truth is she willing to go? Because I know for a fact, neither of us has told a single soul about our recent nuptials.

I lean back in my seat, peeking at Grey's game in front of him while I pretend not to be overly curious about the conversation about to take place.

The blonde bombshell who is my wife steps outside. I take a quick glance at her appearance and try not to chuckle. Yeah, she looks good in professional attire with a skirt that hugs her curves and a blouse that cuts just low enough to tease yet isn't indecent. But the look isn't her. Not even close. Calla is too casual for whatever job she's apparently working at.

"He… I… we…"

"He has a room, Calla. A whole house with space to share."

The pleading in Simon's voice gets to me. I'm the softie in the group; there is no doubt about it. I can't leave the man hanging. He needs backup and fuck it. If anything, I'm a phenomenal friend.

"I just bought a new house, Calla. The basement is a walk-out, so you don't even have to see me if you don't want to. The kitchen and laundry are all we would share, and even then, I'm willing to make a schedule, so we don't run into each other."

She stares at me with a blank expression. "Wow, that sounds *so* inviting."

I almost—*almost* toss my hands up again.

This is a lose-lose situation.

But hell, I tried.

"Alright, well, I should be going. You know where I live if you change your mind."

"Calla, take the offer," Simon says. "I don't want this hiccup to be how you start things off in Wind Valley. The new job was good today, yeah?"

Oh, smooth change in subject. Get her onto something she's more comfortable talking about. Damn he's good.

She nods but doesn't say anything.

"This is only temporary," Simon says, watching Grey as he heads into the house.

I don't really care about her job, but on instinct, I can't help myself. "Where are you working?"

She glares at me. "None of your business."

Simon chuckles. "Oh no, I know that tone. Do you hate it already?"

"I didn't say that."

"Should we make a bet on if you can keep this one longer than a month?"

He bumps elbows with her, and she smiles, as if this is a simple brother and sister teasing act.

Again, I just can't help myself. "No one likes to keep you around that long, huh? Makes sense."

She mock laughs at me and then flips me the bird.

"With as feisty as she can be, you'd think that, but alas, my sister is a free spirit who can't be bothered to make a commitment."

"I make commitments," Calla argues.

"Name one," Simon argues back.

"I…"

He gives her about thirty seconds. "Exactly, you don't stick to anything. Ever. You can't help it. You don't know how to pick one thing and stick to it."

"I can" is the only rebuttal she has.

Simon chuckles. "Well, when it happens, I can't wait to see it. For now, I won't hold my breath."

A loud bang from upstairs makes us jump. Simon rushes into the house, leaving Calla and me alone.

She glares at me, and I just keep smiling.

"This makes sense now," I say. "You rushed into marrying me. Now you're rushing to divorce me."

She swats my shoulder, quickly grabbing my shirt and yanking me close. "Keep your voice down."

I hear her warning, but my gaze drops to her plump pink lips. Fuck. I remember kissing them. I want to do it again. I just don't want to get a black eye in the process.

She notices me looking and shoves me back.

A slow smile creeps onto the lips I was just fantasizing about. "If you want a divorce, I'll give you one, but it won't be my choice."

I laugh so hard my eyes begin to water.

"All because of what your brother just said?" I clarify. She's really going to stay married to me to prove a point?

"No."

"Sure. But that's where this gets tricky. I'm not asking for a divorce."

She holds her gaze and narrows her eyes. "Well, neither am I."

I step closer.

"Calla, if you don't file the papers, that means we're staying married."

"Unless you file them." She grins.

"We both know that won't happen. I told you. My family is all about marriage and making it work. So, if I'm married," —I lean in close, so close my lips almost brush her cheek when I speak— "which I am, to you, I have no choice but to make it work." I lean away.

She huffs, shoving me back into my seat, and goes back inside. I follow her.

I might be a little twisted, but getting Calla worked up is a turn-on for me.

"Do you want to load your stuff in my Forerunner now or later?"

"Screw you, Beck."

"I mean, it's a com—"

She slides the patio door closed before I can finish my sentence. I let out a loud laugh and reach for the handle.

Well, I guess that's that. She's not divorcing me to make a point to her family, and I'm not divorcing her because of mine.

This should be fun.

CHAPTER FIVE
CALLA

When I got fired this morning—let go or *absorbed* or whatever you want to call it—I thought for sure I'd hit rock bottom. Well, turns out, there was another level for me to drop.

"I can't believe I'm here," I say and flop onto Beck's couch.

Oh, damn it! It's comfy as hell.

Ugh. I don't want to like anything about this situation.

"Neither can I," he grunts and walks into the kitchen.

He grabs a water and joins me in the living room. "Oh, no, no thank you, Beck, I didn't want a beverage or anything."

He side-eyes me with a swig and shrugs.

I sigh heavily so he knows how irritated I am.

"I didn't offer you a drink because I assumed you'd have a lot of heavy lifting to do what with my front door wide open and all your things you still have in your car."

"Oh, forgive me if I'm mentally drained after the day from

hell and having to temporarily live under that same roof as you."

I can't pinpoint the exact moment in my life when I decided he wasn't my favorite person. Seeing as he's my older brother's best friend, it isn't as if we had a class together during school or something as kids where he embarrassed me. No, I actually had a class with his little sister, Ava. Talk about total opposite siblings. She's so sweet and funny, and Beck is… he's too cocky. And the worst part about it, he knows how charming and good-looking he is and makes it work for him.

He grunts. "The day from hell? I wouldn't think having a new job and a warm place to lay your head at night is a bad thing. Some people don't have either."

"Shit."

I cover my eyes with my arm and curl into the fetal position.

"What?" Beck steps toward me. "Are you okay?"

"No, I'm not okay. I live with one of those guys. The positive ones. The ones who think we should be grateful for everything we have because there's *always* someone less fortunate. Makes me sick."

It really doesn't, but anything that involves Beck just annoys me.

Surprisingly, my statement earns me a chuckle.

"What?"

"Nothing," he answers with another sip.

"Not nothing. Clearly something."

"Really, it's nothing." He stands and heads back for the kitchen.

"For fuck's sake, Beck, spit it out."

"I just didn't know you were this dramatic."

"I am not dramatic."

He smirks.

"You're a bit dramatic, and you're definitely acting a bit immature."

My mouth drops open, and I huff. "You did not just—"

I pause midsentence when it clicks. Fuck me, he's right.

I groan and stomp out the door.

I can't even with him. My life is complicated right now, and no matter how hard I try, a civil conversation with Beck Robertson will not happen.

"You know," he says, leaning in his front doorway, arms and ankles crossed, "instead of marching out like a madwoman, you could have said, 'sorry, Beck, you're right. It's been a long day, and I'm taking it out on you. My apologies. Would you kindly help me with my things?'"

I roll my eyes and open my trunk to get my pillows and the clothes I managed to salvage that weren't left on the floor of my room at my brother's house.

"In all seriousness, though," Beck says, walking down the sidewalk, "can I help you?"

"No."

"Calla, come on. I'm just teasing."

"I don't need your help, and you were not teasing. You may have said it in a teasing tone, but you meant it. You think I'm immature and dramatic."

His hands go up in surrender.

"You're right. I'm sorry. That was uncalled for."

I pause in gathering my things and look over the top of my Honda at him. I know what he's up to. Next, he's going to point out how easy it was for him to apologize and turn it into some teaching lesson about how this will be easier for the both of us if we come to some sort of truce. Nope. Not falling for it.

I'm smarter than he gives me credit for.

"What?" he asks with another smirk.

"Get it out."

He shakes his head. "Get what out?"

"Your whole 'look at how easy that was for me to apologize' lesson you want to teach me."

His grin widens, and his aqua eyes land on me. My breath hitches.

I know, I know, but hell, just because he annoys the everloving shit out of me doesn't mean I don't think he's attractive.

I married the man, after all.

God, this is just so complicated.

I calm my breathing as he walks toward me, slowly. He moves in a way that's not supposed to be sexy at all as he takes the box I'm holding up against the car with my knee. With the box tucked under his arms, he leans in. "If I wanted to teach you a lesson, Calla, it wouldn't be in the driveway talking about apologies."

Don't ask him where it would be. Don't do it.

"And where else would you teach me?"

He inhales deeply, blowing out his breath over my neck. "Somewhere private, Calla. Is that what you want to hear?"

Yes.

No!

I quickly gain my composure and step back, stacking another box on the one in his hands so he can't see my blushing cheeks.

"I want you to take these inside while I go to my room and change out of these work clothes."

"That's a good private place."

"Beck!"

His laughter follows me into the house.

"Why don't you come with me to Tobias's for dinner? He's grilling, and I know for a fact that your brother and Grey will be there. Nora and Greer, too."

Right, my two best friends. Ex-best friends, since neither of them could offer me a place to stay. To their credit, Willa is happily in love with Zane, and they need their privacy, and Greer's apartment is too small for two people. I can't really be mad at them—it just sucks.

"Ha, right, the two of us, showing up together like a couple of friends who get along. Ha. Ha. Ha."

Beck heads down the stairs with my stuff, so I follow him.

"We aren't friends, Calla."

"Don't I know it?"

"We're husband and wife."

I pause in the hallway outside what I assume is going to be my room since that's where Beck took my boxes.

Asking for a divorce is on the tip of my tongue, but I'm all too quickly reminded of my current life predicament. If I want to be free, Beck has to ask for it.

I'm just not sure how to make that happen. Especially when he doesn't want one to begin with.

"Meet me upstairs in the kitchen in fifteen minutes," he says after it's clear I have no rebuttal for his reference to our relationship.

I brush my hair and change into a pair of holey jeans and a Taylor Swift T-shirt before I meet Beck in the kitchen. He isn't there when I show up, so I take a moment to look around.

Oh. My. Gosh. Someone should hire me as an actress, because the amount of smiling and oohs and ahhs I've had to hold back after seeing all of Beck's house is insane. It's not my first time here, but shit, I loved it before too.

The walls are off-white with big white trim, the kind you'd see in older houses. The main wall in his living room has a gray-and-white marble fireplace with floor-to-ceiling bookshelves on each side of it. The rounded arches into each room that don't have a door are to die for, and the light stained wood floors are so clean I could eat off them.

He had to have hired someone to decorate and pick out the accents for his house because this place is literally a Pinterest-worthy house. I can't believe I get to live here. And the basement is just as beautiful. I love the walkout French doors. When I was in his backyard this past weekend, I thought, 'Come on. Really? French doors to the upper deck and basement walkout and French doors to the lower patio— is that necessary?'

Yes. Yes, it is.

I'm just smoothing my hand over the marble countertops when he walks in, looking like a fucking snack.

I stand ramrod straight.

Wow.

I did not just think that.

I let out a laugh, and Beck glares at me.

"Something funny?"

I pinch my lips together and shake my head.

"No. Let's go."

I walk out of the house faster than a sinner in church on Sunday.

What has gotten into me?

I'm more adult than this. I swear.

I walk around to the passenger side of Beck's SUV, doing my best not to roll my eyes at whatever poison is clearly in the air of the most perfect house, and I feel him walking behind me.

I spin quickly. "What are you doing?"

His brows dip a little in confusion. "What do you mean?"

"Um, you're like right behind me."

"Well, if you would move, I would move, and we could get going."

"That still doesn't answer my question. Why are you this close to me?"

He makes a grunt sound and says, "I'm opening your door, Calla. What did you think I was doing?"

"Well, you just never know with you," I say in response.

He does exactly as he said he was going to do and then, as soon as I'm in, he closes the door and walks around the front to his side.

Beck Robertson just opened the door for me.

Beck. Robertson.

I keep my eyes focused out the front window as he backs out.

Now that I think about it, I'm not so sure any guy has ever opened the door for me.

I chance a glance at Beck and then shift to look out my window.

I have no idea how to get him to ask for a divorce, but I sure as hell know one thing.

I cannot fall for my husband.

CHAPTER SIX

CALLA - VEGAS

I feel like I'm floating.

"Shot, please." I hold up a finger, and the bartender pours two more glasses.

"Calla, this has to be the last one."

"Lightweight?"

"No." Beck groans. "Just not stupid."

I'd already planned for it to be my last. I'm at the point now where everything is perfect. I'm buzzed and happy and relaxed but can totally go to bed without spinning. Beck doesn't need to know that, though.

"So, why didn't you find something to do with Simon and Grey tonight?" Beck asks. "I'm sure their company would be more fun than mine."

"Everyone's company is more fun than yours."

He tilts his drink at me and takes a sip.

I fight back my smile.

Bickering and quick comebacks are a total turn on of mine, but Beck doesn't need to know that.

He looks sharp tonight.

Dark wash jeans and a black button-down. His hair is always styled and clean-cut, and his beard is also so groomed that I bet it's soft to the touch.

Maybe I did have one too many shots.

Still, as much as I can't stand the man, he's beautiful.

"Can I buy you a drink?" a drunk man slurs, bumping into me and flashing me a smile. He looks half asleep with one eye open, and the tequila on his breath is about to make me puke.

"No, thanks."

I turn to face Beck squarely. He's laughing.

That's the third drunk man to come up to me.

"This is funny to you? Aren't you supposed to be like all 'don't touch, her she's my best friend's sister?'"

Beck laughs harder.

"If one gives you more than a bump on the shoulder right there," he touches me softly, "yeah, sure."

I narrow my gaze and sip my mule.

"That's how it starts."

"Calla, these guys are harmless."

"And idiots. Do they really think I'd go for them all drunk? Men are stupid."

"Is that why you're single?"

"Wouldn't you like to know?"

Beck nods with another drink and starts to play with his napkin.

Okay, Calla. He's just making conversation. It's more than you usually get, so maybe give him a bone, yeah?

"I, ugh, I'm pretty picky with guys."

"As you should be."

I glance at him because I'm unsure of how to respond to a kind comment from him.

"Maybe it's because my reading history has filled my mind with fantasies of how a man should treat a woman."

"Or," Beck says without missing a beat, "those books are making you realize your worth."

Jesus. Two for two here.

"I guess. I mean, maybe it's not too much to ask for a guy to hold a door for you or to randomly ask how your day is because he thought of you or to be proud to call you his girlfriend or be happy to see you every single day."

I take a breath. Beck is watching me.

"What?"

He shakes his head. "I've never heard you talk so much without yelling at me. It's nice."

"Don't get used to it," I say, and he chuckles. Which, in turn, makes me smile. This drink should probably be my last.

"Finding the right person is hard. You'll find him, Calla."

"Oh shit, are we friends now?"

My stomach flutters. I'll never forget the day I met Beck. My brother brought him over after school, and he was dreamy. Oh, I thought highly of him up until that day in high school.

"No, but I get it. Falling in love is hard," he says.

"So hard."

"Patience to find the right one is hard."

"Very."

"First dates are hard."

"Ugh, first dates are the worst. I'm tired of first dates. At this point, I'd rather just be married and figure it all out from there than go on a first date again."

He lets out a breath.

"Just be married and figure the rest out after that, huh?"

"Yeah, I mean, arranged marriages work out all the time."

They even make TV shows about it now.

"Some don't."

"True, but some do."

"Then try it," he says simply. "Go marry someone."

"Ha, like who? One of the drunk guys who hit on me, or one—"

"These were sent over from that woman," the bartender interrupts and slides another round of drinks and shots in front of us. "She said sorry about her brother hitting on you."

I lean forward to wave a thank-you and then grab my shot.

"Cheers," I say, and we toss back our shots.

"I didn't mean one of those drunk guys," Beck says as the fireball liquid burns down my throat. "I meant me."

CHAPTER SEVEN

BECK

I can't remember the last time I rode in a car with someone, and no one said a single word for the entire drive.

Thankfully, Wind Valley is small enough that even if you're going from one side of town to the other, you can get anywhere in twenty minutes tops.

As soon as I put my car in park outside Tobias's house, Calla jumps out and speed walks inside. I've barely got my seatbelt back in place before she's gone.

I start to get out but stop.

Hell, what if she really hates me? Like seriously wants nothing to do with me. No matter what I do or how hard I try, convincing her to stay married might just be a waste of time.

I let out a sigh and get out.

I have to at least try, but I hate the fact that divorce might be inevitable.

I skip using the front door like Calla did and instead use the side gate. Almost everyone is in the backyard already. Tobias did some new landscaping at the start of summer, so now there's a designated seating area around the firepit. It can fit about twelve people, which is great since our group seems to be growing lately.

I remember when it was just the six of us: Tobias, Simon, Graham, Hero, Zane, and myself. We'd drink cheap booze and plot books until well after midnight. It was how we'd all come up with numerous bestsellers.

Now, BBQs here and there are more of a reason for us all to get together with our busy lives. Tobias holds one annually, so tonight it is. Yeah, we meet weekly to write together, but this night is different. We chill, we relax, we play games and compete for the prize of getting to name someone else's next book. It's just a good time.

I'll admit, with Hero and Nora getting together and then Zane and Willa, adding people has made it more fun. Which, in turn, brought Willa's friend Greer. Then, of course, since Willa is also friends with Calla and the simple fact that she's Simon's sister, it only made sense for her to come too. Simon also brings his son. And we can't forget Tobias's best friend, Natalie. She's been a steady staple since our college years and still is, but we see less of her now that she's dating Griffin. Today, however, she and her boyfriend are in attendance. It's a packed house.

Hell, he's going to need a bigger yard once someone starts having kids.

If I can make it work with Calla, shoot, maybe it'll be us.

"Beer." Tobias shoves one in my chest.

I grunt a little but take it and twist the cap off. He isn't looking at me; he's watching Natalie. She's standing next to Nora, and the two of them are playing cornhole with Griffin and Hero.

"Have you ever thought of telling her how you feel?"

"What are you talking about?" he asks, pulling his gaze from her to me and taking a drink.

"You clearly like Natalie."

He just shakes his head.

"Don't you?"

"I'm not having this conversation again," he says and drops into one of his black Adirondack chairs.

"What are you two gossiping about?" Zane says as he and Simon join us.

"Tobias and Natalie," I say.

Zane and Simon share a look.

"No, we were changing the subject," Tobias cuts us all off.

Simon chuckles. "Fine by me. I came out here to ask Beck how things went with getting my sister moved in this afternoon."

"You and Calla are living together?" Zane just about spits his beer out.

"It hasn't even been a day, and fine, I guess. We rode here together and didn't kill each other. Seems like steady progress."

"Oh, cute," Tobias says. "It's like you're a couple."

"No, it's not like that."

Well, it is, but none of my friends know that. But it's also not because she doesn't want this.

Fuck. I can't keep my life straight right now. I need my computer to sort this out.

"Oh, you can live with a woman and be friends, but I can't even look at one without you all jumping down my throat about it being more."

My friends and I share a guilty look.

He has a point. I guess since Natalie and Griffin have been dating for more than a year now, maybe he doesn't like her more than as a friend. It's possible he's just protective. They have been friends for about as long as our group has been.

"Sorry," I say with sincerity. "I just always assumed, and that was wrong of me."

"Oh fuck, don't go all soft of me now. I'm just telling you how it is."

"Hey, what are you guys doing?" Natalie pops up next to me with Griffin right behind her.

"I have to take a piss," Tobias says and jumps up, practically jogging to the house.

It's official: I'll never understand how he and Natalie work.

"Talking about how my sister moved into Beck's place today."

"Oh my gosh." Natalie beams. "I had no idea you were dating. Wow, I know I've been more absent lately than normal." She rubs Griffin's arms and smiles at him. He leans down to kiss her. "But I can't believe I missed that."

"You didn't," I answer as Simon chuckles.

"My basement flooded, and she just needs a place to stay. These two are the furthest thing from dating."

I almost choke on my beer.

"Oh, well, that's still fun. A roommate. I've only ever lived with Nora back in college, and I loved every minute of it. I sometimes miss it."

Tobias returns, a new beer in hand.

"Babe, if you want a roommate, why don't you move in with me?" Griffin asks her.

Oh shit.

Shit.

Simon and Zane both look like a deer in headlights, no doubt I have the same look on my face, and Tobias, well, looks like he needs another beer. He's gone before Natalie has an answer.

"Are you being serious?" she asks him.

"Of course. I'm crazy about you."

I do my best not to smile. Don't get me wrong, I don't think any of this is funny or a good thing for Tobias. No, it's more like this is exactly how I get inspiration for writing. Watching people. And this right here is gold for my plotting brain.

I need a story, stat, and friends to lovers just might be what I need. A love triangle perhaps.

"Alright then, let's do it," Natalie answers and then squeals when he wraps her in a hug.

I meet Simon's eyes, and he mouths *holy fuck.*

Laughter breaks up the intensity of the moment, and we all turn. Willa and Greer are all in a fit of giggles, while Calla looks annoyed.

Ha. I bet she just told them about our new roommate situation. Which, coincidentally enough, did not go as cheery as the one in front of me. At least I have both options to consider if I put it in a story.

"Thank you, by the way," Simon says next to me. "I don't think I said that earlier."

"I think you did, but no problem."

He chuckles. "I just hope the next few weeks aren't too bad for you. She can be a handful. Growing up was fun as hell when I think about it, but that's because Calla has always been full of surprises. I'd love for her to settle down and figure out life, but honestly, if she did, I'm not sure she'd be the same sister I love so much."

"Settle down and figure out life?" I question back to him. "She seems fine to me."

"I don't mean it in a bad way," he corrects quickly. "But she turns thirty next month. Everyone else here tonight has a steady job, owns or rents their own place, and has direction. Calla isn't quite there yet."

She must sense that we're looking at her because she glances over her shoulder and locks her gaze on mine. She doesn't wrinkle her nose or roll her eyes; she just watches me.

"She just needs someone or something to guide her where to go, I think."

I know what it's like to be a big brother and worry about your sister, but my back stiffens as an overwhelming irritation at how he's talking about her consumes me. I keep my voice as calm as I can.

"Your sister is doing just fine, Simon. Have a little faith in her, yeah?"

He stops the beer bottle at his lips and narrows his gaze.

I expect him to say something right away, but he doesn't.

"Dad!" Grey runs up, holding an old-fashioned root beer bottle that looks almost like the one his dad is holding.

Simon's confused expression morphs into a wide smile.

"What is that?" he asks.

"Greer brought them for me." Grey answers as she joins us.

"Sorry, I hope that's okay. I just saw them at the store before I came here and thought it would be a fun idea for him."

"That was really sweet of you, Greer. Thank you."

"I'm going to go show Aunt Calla," he says quickly, tilting his drink back the same as his dad.

"Umm," Greer starts as she eyes the father and son duo. "Did I just start a bad habit?"

I chuckle at the same time as Simon.

"You did great," he says. "But I might remind him that he can only have one until he eats."

Simon brushes a hand against Greer's lower back as he passes her.

It's brief, but I catch it. A small grin tugs her lips.

Her eyes dart to mine, and I look away quickly.

Hell, look at all this inspiration around me. I should have endless words flowing from my fingers. Being stuck in a new book sucks.

"So, you and Calla, huh?" she asks, taking a seat. I do the same.

"Roommates. Yep," I answer. I'm not sure if Calla has told anyone about Vegas. From the way she pretends it never happened, it's safe to assume that's a no.

"Well," Greer says with a pause. "I think it's great. Maybe by the end of it, you two will actually be friends."

Or something.

"Yeah, maybe."

"Greer!" Willa calls out and waves her hand for her to join her.

"Enjoy your beer," she says, leaving me alone.

I could get up and mingle, but I can see every person here from this spot. I won't lie—as much as I want to relax, I can't stop thinking about this nonexistent book I have. Always thinking about the next book is a weakness of mine. There are so many stories out there to write, but I don't know what mine is. People-watching usually helps.

As I scan the yard, my gaze lands on Calla who, like before, is looking my way.

Oh, the things I would give to know what's going on inside that head of hers. Once and only once did she let me in, and hell, that's all it took for me to become interested as more than a friend.

I grin and wink.

She flips me the bird.

I let out a laugh and shake my head.

The next few weeks are going to be so much fun.

CHAPTER EIGHT

BECK - VEGAS

Holy shit, did I just propose to Calla Stone?

Fuck. I think I did.

I stare at the golden liquid in front of me, waiting for either her to say something or me to start freaking out and saying all the wrong things to take back the words that just tumbled off my lips.

Except, I'm not freaking out.

I'm fully aware of what I just said, and I… I don't want to take it back.

It is crazy. But honestly, what she said a few minutes ago is exactly how I feel.

I'm done having firsts for everything. I know what I want. By the sounds of it, Calla wants the same thing.

Am I going about this wrong? Also yes. But hell, this is how all the great love stories start.

Oh shit, does this make me look desperate?

"Let's go dancing," Calla says, waving the bartender down and asking for the check.

"Dancing?"

I grab the check that appears between us, swatting Calla's hand out of the way.

She studies me for a moment, as if she is trying to decide whether she's going to argue with me, but then she nods.

"Yes, dancing."

I drop some cash on the bar top and stand. "Look, Calla, I didn't mean to make you uncomfortable with my statement. I apologize if that's what happened."

She stands, too, and grabs my hand to pull me behind her.

"I just want to dance, Beck. So let's do that."

I follow her out of the bar and into the casino, weaving through the slot machines and pop-up stores until we reach the glass doors that lead back to the Strip.

"Where are we going?" I ask as the cool night air surrounds us.

"Oh, that feels good." She stops walking, looks up at the sky, and closes her eyes. "It was hot in there."

"Yeah, maybe too hot." I grab the back of my neck. I'm not drunk. Not by any means. Buzzed, sure, but not drunk, and Calla… fuck, she looks good. The way her dress hugs her ass makes me feel like it's illegal to even be looking at her.

She starts to laugh, and the sound makes my dick twitch.

My gaze flashes to hers.

She's grinning because she caught me. It makes me smile too.

"Now that we've had a moment to cool down, do you still think we should get married?" she asks.

"Yes," I answer without missing a beat.

The answer was a jerk reaction that, oddly, I still stand by.

Yeah, so what if Calla and I have never dated? We have never even kissed or hugged, for that matter.

But I've known her since we were kids. It happens when you grow up in the same town. So I feel like I know her well enough to know that, despite our differences, this feels right.

"Okay."

She starts walking, so I follow.

"We're doing this, just like that?"

"No." She laughs. "Let's see if we can hang out for the night first. You know, make sure we don't kill each other before the sun comes up. It's weird, but right now, I think I might like you."

She trips, so I reach out to grab her hand. She wasn't going to fall, but hell if this isn't a smooth move to touch her.

She studies our hands as I link our fingers together.

"Call me crazy," I say. "But I think I might like you too."

CHAPTER NINE

BECK

I toss my stress ball against the wall and then catch it. I do it again and again and again.

What should this heroine's career goals be?

She could be a doctor.

Toss ball. Catch.

A chef.

Toss ball. Catch.

An athlete.

Toss ball and—

"What the ever-loving hell are you doing in here?"

The ball smacks me in the forehead as I dodge out of my chair at the outburst that just came through my office door.

Calla is standing in the doorway, her light hair a curly mess as it falls over her shoulders, framing her face.

She's got on a pair of polka dot pajama shorts and a tank top that cuts off at her belly button, showing the smallest amount of skin to tease a guy just right.

Slowly, a grin takes over my lips. If I recall on the night

we got married, she reminded me multiple times how my sly grin makes her want to crawl into my lap.

I know the moment her eyes land on my mouth. She switches her stance, crosses the opposite leg in front of the other, and glares at me.

"I know what you're doing."

"Do you now?"

She nods. "Mm-hmm. It's not going to work."

I tilt my head. "No?"

Her expression switches like a light switch from annoyed to flirtatious.

"Well," she steps into my office. "Unless…"

I swallow. She's calling my bluff. Except it isn't really a bluff. Yes, we are married. Yes, we have kissed, but the rest of it? Not so much.

She runs her finger over my collarbone and then stands behind me to whisper in my ear, "We are married, after all. Shouldn't we get the reward for that tiny fact?"

I lick my lips and close my eyes. An image of all the things I want to do to her flash through my mind. On my desk, on the floor, in this chair, up against the wall… the list goes on.

"We are." I clear my throat.

I reach for her leg, but she backs up.

"Too bad I don't like you."

My hands drop to my thighs and my chin to my chest.

"Calla, you know I find you sexy as hell, right?"

"I do. Now, why are you throwing a ball against my wall?"

Shit, I forgot that was her room now.

"Sorry about that. It's part of my process."

She nods slowly. "Well, find a new wall while I'm here, please."

She turns for the door, and I have to close my eyes at the sight of her ass cheeks giving the sexiest peek-a-boo from the bottom of her shorts.

It's no secret that I find Calla extremely attractive. Despite her dislike of me, I don't mind Calla, and if we'd met on different terms, and took the proper steps to become a married couple, I truly believe we would be happy together.

Perhaps making two fictional characters fall in love isn't where my focus should be. Yes, I want this book/movie deal, but I also want a marriage that works. I have a marriage now —I just need to find a way to make it work.

So writing the story on how to make fictional people fall in love might need to go on the back burner. Instead, I need to focus on the real thing.

How can I make Calla fall in love with me enough to stay married?

CHAPTER TEN

CALLA

I've officially lived with Beck Robertson for a whole week now. Also, for a whole week, I've faked having to work at 7 a.m. just so I don't see him in the morning. In reality, I've gone to Willa's new health and fitness studio downtown to hang out.

It's worked well so far. I just have one little problem. Tomorrow is Saturday.

"So, pretend to sleep in," Willa says, setting up her camera and workout studio for today's video.

"Or find a new hobby," Greer, her business partner, adds as she shifts the ring light.

Me, I grab another donut and force eat the gluten-free, sugar-free disappointment.

"I have a million hobbies as it is."

"And none of them will get you out of the house?" Willa asks.

"Probably, but the thing is, I really, really just want to snuggle up with my coffee and a book right on that fluffy circle chair thing he has in the basement. It's like a cloud of pillows. I could just read and sleep all day long."

The three of us laugh. "So I'm going to say it's safe to assume you haven't told him how much you love living at his house."

"God no," I say and drink my water. "I'm still in shock at the entire thing."

I've learned a lot in a week, but the most important thing is that Beck is the male version of me.

It's both glorious and annoying at the same time.

He never leaves clothes in the wash. He folds them right out of the dryer and puts them away. He picks up the house every single night before he goes to bed, including doing all the dishes. I'm almost certain he vacuums every day. He lines his shoes up at the door, and the list goes on.

To be honest, if he couldn't speak, he'd be my dream guy.

He loves a clean and organized house, and if I ever came out of my room, he'd know I do too. However, I don't plan for him to get to know me at all. I won't be there long.

"Maybe you should tell him," Willa offers. "Finding out the two of you have something in common could be good. Might make the time you live together bearable."

I shake my head.

"Remind us again why you can't be friends with him." Greer crosses her arms.

I do this frowning lip thing. They don't need all the details. The fewer people who know, the better.

"You're not telling us something," Willa says, stepping up next to Greer.

"I … I'm … I am." I say it slowly, as if the weird word mix-up didn't just give me away. "I. Am."

Both of them continue to stare at me, so I pretend to be useful and straighten a straight picture on the wall.

"You remember I lived with you in college, right?" Willa speaks up.

"So?"

"So, what aren't you telling me?"

I fake laugh.

"We lived together one summer between semesters. It doesn't mean you—" I stop, turn around, and they're both shaking their heads.

"Better stop while you're ahead." Greer chuckles. "Just spill. It's us. We're the last people to judge you."

Greer is right: if I share this with anyone, it would be them. Maybe she's right.

My hesitation is enough time for them to both go nuts.

"This is good, isn't it?"

"Is this the real reason you moved here?"

"Does it involve Beck?"

"Did you sleep with him?"

I lick my lips and take a breath.

"First of all, no," I say with a hand on my heart. "I did not sleep with him, thank you very much. And second, I moved here because I wanted to. End of story."

"So it does involve Beck!" Greer shouts. Willa giggles.

"Glad you two were listening."

"Just tell us."

"Alright." I stretch my neck side to side as if I'm prepping for a fight.

This is happening. I'm doing it. I'm telling them. Maybe they can help.

"Beck and I got married in Vegas when the guys were there a couple months ago."

Silence.

Complete silence.

"This is a joke, right?" Greer asks first.

"Nope. Not a joke."

Willa opens her mouth but then closes it. She does this a few more times before she takes a seat in one of the chairs near the front window.

"You. Married. Beck."

I nod.

"In Vegas."

I nod again.

"How in the hell did this happen?" she finally manages to get out with a lot less shock than her first two statements.

I spin and march to the chair behind her desk, plopping into it and covering my face with my hands. I don't know where or how to begin. I keep playing that night over and over, and I just can't figure out what part of me didn't know when it was time to call it quits.

"It doesn't matter how it happened. What matters is that I need it to end, and I can't do it."

"What do you mean, you can't do it?"

"I mean that everyone knows me as someone who can't commit. Even I know it."

Neither of them argues.

"So, I won't be the first one to bow out."

"I'm sure Beck will. He probably just hasn't asked because he wants to find a way to let you down easy."

"Wrong. Beck told me that marriage is basically sacred to

his family and that no one has ever been divorced. He refuses to be the first."

I leave out the part where he also said two people make this pact for a reason, and he wants to find out that reason. Of all the boyfriends I've had in my life, I can't believe the one who wasn't even dating me to begin with is the one who wants to put in the most effort.

"So neither of you will file?"

"Correct."

Greer thinks her next words over. "Are you not asking because you want to prove to you that you can commit or because you want to prove it to someone else? I think this situation should be excluded from proving anything to anyone, and if you want to file, you should."

"Maybe a little of both."

"So you're both going to be stubborn about it?" Willa asks.

"Seems that way. However," I say with a little raised pitch and a smile, "if he asks for a divorce, I can agree and then it's over. I just can't be the one to quit first."

Willa tries not to smile.

"What?"

"Nothing."

"Say it."

"I just think that you know these guys. Being married to Beck might not be that bad. Maybe give him a chance."

"And if it really sucks, just drive him insane till he can't stand you anymore," Greer adds. Willa groans.

"That," I point at Greer. "That's the kind of support I'm looking for. Let's talk more about driving Beck bonkers till he asks for a divorce."

"This is a bad idea," Willa warns. "Beck is a nice guy, and he's super cute. And—" She covers her face with her hands. "Oh gosh, I probably shouldn't repeat this, but Zane once told me that he heard Beck and a girl he picked up while they were at a signing having sex once. Said the whole thing inspired an entire book."

I do everything in my power to keep my face neutral. The last thing I need to know is how amazing Beck is in bed. What I need is to not think of him as anything other than the enemy.

"Now that you mention it," Greer chimes in again, "when he writes enemies to lovers, Beck's sex scenes are fire."

She fans her face, and I roll my eyes. I have to. She's not wrong. Beck writes them better than any of the guys. I'd never share that, of course, because to anyone who asks, I've never read his books.

But he does.

"I still like your first idea better." I grab my phone and pull out the notes list app. "Let's brainstorm ideas."

With heavy sighs, both girls just nod.

"Well, what's he like?" Greer asks. "What would drive him nuts?"

I think for a second and smile like the Cheshire cat. Considering Beck and my brother have been friends since junior high, I know Beck a lot better than I like to admit.

And if Beck is the female me, if I hate it, he will too. This is going to be easy.

I put my phone back in my purse.

"I think Operation Drive Beck Bonkers won't need that much planning. I already have ideas."

I let out a long breath and nod.

I can do this. I'll have him counting down the days until I sign those papers, and I'm out of his life for good. He'll practically pack my things for me.

I look up to find two waiting faces.

"What?" I ask.

"Um, we still want to know how you two got married."

I shake my head.

"You'll tell us, eventually. Just tell us now."

Damn. They know me too well.

"Do you want the short version or the long version?"

"The long one." Greer takes the chair next to Willa.

"Don't leave out a single detail," Willa adds.

"Okay, do you have wine? I might need it for this."

Willa squeals. "Man, I wish Beck was here for this. I'd love to get his side too."

I scratch my nose to hide my grin. I have a feeling I know exactly how his side of things went. Like I said, I know him better than I care to admit.

CHAPTER ELEVEN
CALLA - VEGAS

The farther into the club Beck and I get, the louder the music grows. We follow a long dark hallway toward flashing lights altering between purple, blue, green, yellow, and red. At the end of the hallway, we come to a large, open room packed with bodies. I step to the rail and look down at the dance floor. It's a three-level club, and we're on the second floor, with the dance floor at the center of the first. Dancers in sparkling silver outfits dance on individual platforms in each corner of the space. Booths with personal waitresses—I assume this is the bottle service the guy at the front tried to sell us on—line each level of the club.

"This is insane," Beck says behind me. His front brushes my backside, which causes my heart to race.

Until Beck made the comment to get married, I'd never looked at him as more than this hot guy my brother was friends with, but something, I can't even tell you what, but something from that one remark flipped a switch inside me.

It flipped so hard that I had to get us out of there. I had to get air and think. I want to say yes. But that would be crazy.

We were just caught in drinks and those random dudes hitting on me and needed a change of scenery.

So I thought.

Beck leans in and his clean linen smell, which I never thought was sexy till now, consumes me as his warm breath hits my ear. "Let's go to the dance floor."

Holy hell. Someone's warm breath against any part of my face shouldn't make my thighs jerk together.

"Okay," I basically yell so he can hear me.

Like before, he grabs my hand, and we head down the closest set of steps.

We shimmy our way to an open spot. Well, I shouldn't say open because no matter where we stand, our bodies are smashed together. Beck is behind me, so he wraps his arms around my waist to hold me close. Instantly, our hips fall into rhythm together. I'm not sure how much time passes before I spin around to face him, my wrists locking behind his neck.

"What?" I ask. "Why are you smiling at me like that?"

"I'm just... we should have started getting along a long time ago."

"Who know all we needed was to get a few drinks in our bodies and—"

Cold, sticky liquid splashes in my face.

"What the fuck?" Beck shouts and shoves the guy next to me.

"Chill out, man, it was an accident."

"Back up," Beck says, stepping between me and the guy whose drink is now covering the left side of my hair and face.

The guy holds his hands up and does just that. Once he's far enough away to Beck's liking, Beck turns around.

"Are you okay?"

Instead of answering, I burst into laughter. "And now you're ready to beat someone up for me. Wow, we have come a long way in the last three hours."

A cocky grin touches his lips as his thumb swipes under my left eye. "You've got a little makeup right here."

My smile drops as I grab my clutch and flip it open so I can see myself with the built-in mini mirror. He's right—black mascara is smeared on my face.

"Still want to marry me?" I tease.

He smirks and then nods. "Yeah, a little makeup isn't going to scare me."

The way he answers, so carefree and relaxed, makes me pause. I enjoy this new playful side of him. We aren't actually talking about getting married. I'm pretty sure at this point, it's a running joke. My heart flutters a little at the amount of flirting we're doing just to keep the joke running. Tonight is a good night. I'll keep playing because I'm having fun, and who knows? Maybe this turn of events could turn into a friendship for Beck and me.

"What about last weekend when I was staying with my brother, and you caught me in my ratty sweats and holey T-shirt?"

He nods as if he's thinking it over.

"Well, if I can't stand looking at them and you're my wife, I guess I'd just take them off."

My stomach flutters, and I have to look away. I'm not an idiot. I know I'm blushing right now. Like before, I have to pinch my thighs together. Beck is making my mind venture to places it really, and I mean really, shouldn't.

"Noted" is the response I finally come up with.

Beck smirks again, and I shove him back. "Stop doing that."

He laughs and pulls me closer, his arms looping around my lower back.

"I can't help it. My future wife brings out a side of me I didn't even know existed."

"Hmm, a good side or a bad side?"

A serious expression crosses his eyes.

"You tell me. Do you want it to be good, or do you want it bad?"

I shake my head, clearly growing used to these comments of his.

"Bad. I want it bad."

I meant it as a joke, you know? To put him on edge or make him feel as turned on as I am with no reward in sight.

Beck, however, has different plans.

Instead of replying with words, he jerks me closer.

I can feel his erection pressing against my lower abs, and I gasp.

The noise is quickly silenced by his lips against mine.

The hand that was at my lower back is now threading through my hair, and his other hand is cupping my ass. My hands are grasping his neck as if my life depends on this kiss. As if it depends on his tongue tangling with my own, breathing life back into my body.

Kissing Beck is out of this world. His moan of approval vibrates across our lips, and he grinds against me.

"Let's get out of here."

I nod, never breaking the kiss.

Swiftly, he turns his hand in mine and pulls me behind him out of the club.

"Where are we going?" I ask.

"It's a surprise."

"I don't like surprises."

"You'll like this one."

"Probably not. Now tell me."

Even though I don't like surprises, I'm still smiling. I was just kissing Beck, and I plan to do more of it.

"Are you always this stubborn?"

I nod. "Oh, yeah, and if we're married, you'll learn all my other annoying traits."

"I think I'd survive."

"Only one way to find out," I tease as he comes to a stop in front of a little chapel inside the same hotel as the club.

"Here," he says. "Are you ready?"

CHAPTER TWELVE
CALLA

Today is day one of Drive Beck Bonkers. I figure the first full day I have to be around him is the best day to get this started. If I play my cards right, maybe I'll be divorced by the end of next week.

I can hear him in the kitchen making a smoothie.

I bounce up the steps with a smile on my face. He looks up almost instantly.

Here goes nothing.

"Morning," he says. Shit.

Beck I was prepared for. Annoyingly tight T-shirt-wearing Beck. Not shirtless and ripped abs and backside Beck. Is that required for a writer? The whole chiseled thing?

Hell.

"Calla, are you okay?"

I pick my jaw up and nod.

"Totally, bug."

"Bug?" His left brow rises.

I just smile and walk past him.

"Yep."

He lets out a slight chuckle and turns on the blender.

Good. Yes. I need noise to block out the thoughts in my mind.

Bug. Was that really all I could come up with?

The blender shuts off, and he points to the table where a card and flowers sit.

"That's for you."

"Me?"

He nods.

"Who are they from?"

He drinks his smoothie right from the blender cup and points to his chest.

"You got me flowers?" I turn so he can't see the small smile that touches my lips. I can't remember the last time someone bought me flowers. "What's it for?"

"Read the card."

I reach slowly. I don't want to look as eager as I feel.

Congrats on week one at your new job. Enjoy your day off and a coffee with me.

~Beck~

A gift card to Love's a Brewing drops from the card.

Wow. This is sweet. Simple. I hate that I like it and that he's gifting me for something I don't have.

"Thank you."

I don't know what else to say, so it's a good thing he replies.

"You're welcome. Any plans today?" Beck asks.

"Nope."

Annoy you and read. Get a coffee now.

"I was thinking of heading home for the afternoon, grabbing dinner, and then coming back later. Do you want to join me?"

"Aren't you home now?"

"I meant to Melody. I've been meaning to make the drive to see my parents. With my sister and I both living in Wind Valley now, my parents get lonely."

"You want to go to Melody together?"

He nods. "Why not?"

"I don't know. That sounds super couple-y."

"Couple-y? Is that a word?"

"Maybe. You tell me, Mr. Writer."

"I'm not sure it is, but hey, if you have enough confidence, why not use it?"

"O-kay."

"So that's a no on coming with me."

"Yes."

"You don't want to go home?"

"Nope. I have things I need to get done around here."

"You just said you have nothing to do today."

"Nothing that involves you," I clarify. Especially now that he bought me flowers. He can't be nice when I have opposite plans.

He shakes his head. "Fine."

Then he washes his dishes, dries them, and puts them away.

I quickly make some eggs and toast and am about to do

my own dishes. I love it when there are no dishes in the sink, which means Beck does too.

I set my plate and fork down and slowly back up.

God, this is painful.

I make a run for it but crash right into Beck.

"In a hurry?" he asks.

"Yep."

"To do nothing?"

"Yes," I say with a nod. Neither of us has moved.

The rise of his chest brushes against mine.

I suck in a breath and close my eyes. The memory of the first time he kissed me on the dance floor consumes me, and I almost reach for him.

"Calla," he says, his voice dropping deep. The warmth of his breath on my shoulder sends a tingle through my entire body.

As soon as it causes my nipples to harden, I pull it together enough to move from his touch.

"I have to go."

I start to walk out of the kitchen, cringing as I think of my dishes.

I can do it. Plus, it beats running into his stupid hard body again.

I book it downstairs before I can change my mind.

I wait about a half hour, filling the time looking for open jobs before I assume the coast is clear. I grab a book and curl into my new favorite chair and let out a deep breath. This is what I needed; a moment to myself and—

"Oh good, you like the chair."

My eyes spring open. Beck is rounding the corner from the stairs, a pleased smile on his face.

I thought he was leaving. Is he following me?

I feel the scowl on my face tighten. "What are you doing down here?"

He points behind me.

"My office is down here."

Fudge. I knew that.

He nods and walks past me.

That's it? No teasing or anything? Just a normal, calm conversation between two people.

Did he even notice the dirty dishes?

I peek over the back of the chair, but his door is closed now.

So what? We just both hang out in the house like roommates?

Quietly, I sneak up to the kitchen.

The sink is empty. He just did my dishes with no complaints.

I rush back to my spot in the chair and open my book, but I can't focus.

Maybe this is a prank, or maybe I'm sleeping and this whole Beck thing is one big fat dream—but I know it's not. I don't know why this is so hard for me to process. Maybe I'm still a little dumbfounded as to how I got myself into this situation to begin with. The crazy thing is, married or not, my brother's basement flooding would have landed me here anyway. I know it just as much as Beck does.

The dryer dings to let me know my clothes are ready to be folded. As I'm getting up, Beck comes out of his office.

"Is that you?" he asks.

"Yeah, I was doing laundry."

"Clearly." He chuckles. "I have some clothes in the wash,

so let me know when you're done with the dryer." And he goes back to work. He's overly nice today. It's throwing me off.

I open the dryer but pause.

This is another opportunity I can't waste.

But, oh god, this one is going to hurt worse, even if I know he's waiting on me and it'll be worth it.

I hate wrinkled clothes. I can feel myself already stressing out thinking of them being cold when I fold them later.

I close the dryer door with my clothes still inside and return to my chair. I stare at the laundry room door.

"I'm sorry, clothes," I whisper. "I'm sorry you're going to sit there all warm and unfolded and you'll all get wrinkly as you cool down, and I'm not there to fold you and put you where you belong."

I start reading my book. Well, I try. I really can't handle not folding clothes, but sooner or later, Beck is going to come out and want to switch his clothes and he won't be able to. Annoying, right?

Ten excruciating minutes later—yes, I watched the clock— he comes out.

"Dryer all ready?"

"Oh, no, I'll fold my stuff later. I'm reading."

Silence.

I don't even have to pretend to hold back a laugh. I'm disgusted too.

Beck walks over to the dryer without a word and starts to fold my clothes.

I let him too.

It hurts. It hurts so bad.

Letting him fold my laundry wasn't on the list of things I

could do to annoy him, but it is now. Even if I'm concentrating on all the shirts and socks he's folding the wrong way.

I pull out my phone and tap the notes app where I made my Drive Beck Bonkers plan.

I quickly type in this new addition and scan the list:

Gargle mouthwash.

Only cook dinner for one.

Use annoying nickname.

Burp in front of him.

Call or text him constantly.

Be messy.

Wear baggy or unattractive clothes. Figure out his type and do the opposite.

Become a plant lady?

Bring his car home on empty.

As I try to determine the best one to do next, I pull up a group text with Willa and Greer.

Calla: He's folding my clothes.

Willa: What a gentleman!

Calla: No, I left them on purpose so he couldn't do his laundry, and instead he's doing mine for me.

Greer: So you're upset your husband is helping with household chores.

Calla: He's not my husband.

Willa: Legally, he is.

Calla: He also bought me flowers.

Greer: Aww. I don't know him very well, but I think I changed my mind. I vote no sabotage.

Willa: I second this.

Calla: You're supposed to be on my team.

I hear the dryer turn on, so I drop my phone and open the book. Beck doesn't say a word as he passes me. My clothes are in my basket, which he's clearly taking to my room.

I sit up after his office door closes.

He's not even going to comment on it? No sarcastic "Hey, don't be lazy" or "I'm not your slave" or anything? Just… nothing.

Does this man have no standards?

I pull out my list again and delete everything. Clearly, the petty little things won't work. I need to bring out the big guns.

Wish me luck.

CHAPTER THIRTEEN

BECK

My group's writing Wednesdays are starting to stress me out more than they used to.

Calla and I have been living together for two weeks now. It's been… a trip.

"How's living with my sister?" Simon asks as we all pack up our computers. "And don't show Grey your hair, okay? If he sees that you have blue hair, I'll never hear the end of it."

I rub a hand through my Smurf hair. I have no words. No thoughts. I don't even know where to begin when it comes to Simon's sister. Walking around my house to see things moved here and there is one thing. Folding her clothes is one thing. Doing her dishes is one thing. Showing her selfless acts of kindness like my parents would do for each other is all part of my "we are perfect for each other plan"—but this. I blow out a breath. I'm speechless.

This is the fucked-up part: I still want to make this work. I just need to get through whatever this phase is she has going on right now. I mean, what the hell even is it?

"It's fine. Every day is different."

He chuckles a little.

"So really, things are fine with Calla?"

"Yep. Fine. I mean, it would have been cool if you warned me that she hated housework or that she can't cook to save a life." I won't mention the oatmeal concoction thing I found in the fridge from her the other day with a note that read, Enjoy breakfast! For a minuscule second, I thought, hey, maybe she's coming around.

Nope.

"By the way, what was it like never having folded laundry in your house while you were growing up? I can't believe you two lived with clothes stuffed in a drawer, no organization whatsoever."

I shake my head and sling my bag over my shoulder. My mind is blown by these new tidbits I've learned about Calla, but I can move past it. It's just out of the norm for me.

Simon bursts into laughter. "Who are you talking about?"

I glance up into the faces of all my friends.

"Your sister. Calla."

He snorts. "That's not Calla."

"Um, news flash. It is. I live with her."

"Well, that's not the Calla I grew up with. My sister is a clean freak and organization is her thing. She's such a weirdo about everything being in place, she should open her own business. Help others get organized."

This time, it's me who laughs. Hard.

"I think she's playing him," Zane says.

"Yes. I'm here for this," Hero adds.

"Does this mean next time I come over, there won't be dishes and clothes all over the living room?" Graham asks.

Everyone is laughing now.

"So she's fucking with me?"

"She has to be. I can't think of any other reason for her to be like this." He shrugs. "You two hate each other, but this is a new level. Don't worry, I'm only a few weeks out from a working basement and then she'll be out of your hair."

In an instant, the idea of Calla leaving bothers me more than the idea that she's been tricking me this entire time.

"Yeah, she'll be happy to hear it."

Simon stops moving and looks at me. I heard the catch in my voice too.

Lucky for me, he doesn't say anything.

"Anyone have time to read a few chapters of this new WIP I've got?" Graham asks. "I'll have them ready by tomorrow."

"I do," I answer quickly. "I need the inspiration and reading the starting chapters of someone else's work always helps."

"Stuck on a book?" Simon asks.

I nod. "Yeah. When I was solely self-published, I could write anything at any time. Now that I'm hybrid and have a contract to fulfill, it's different. The pressure to keep up takes the fun out of it."

"Is that all it is?"

"Yeah, what else would it be?"

He shrugs. "Maybe having a roommate is throwing you off."

"Perhaps." I smile. "But now that I know she's deliberately trying to drive me insane and I don't have a total whack job for a roommate, I do feel lighter. Inspired even."

"Fuck." Simon chuckles. "Just don't light her on fire or

color her hair. I'm starting to put the pieces together and sense she's the one who did that to you."

"Me too, and no promises." I pat his back and head home.

Now that I'm aware that Calla could be doing all of this to me intentionally, I need to be on my toes.

I peek through my front windshield to view the front of my house.

Shit.

It's dark. It's midday, but the house looks like it's vacant.

What has Calla done now?

I close my eyes, lean back, and grip the steering wheel.

Just because the house is dark doesn't mean that she did anything. Hell, who am I kidding? It all makes sense now. Calla is hell-bent on doing whatever it takes to get me to crack and demand a divorce. The blue hair dye in my shampoo—whatever. Gargling her mouthwash like a fish gasping for air—also fine. It's actually a bit comical. The pink frilly pillows and cushy throw blankets that make me sweat after five minutes of use to clearly signify that a woman lives here—who cares?

It was the pickles in my tuna sandwich and the diet chips that almost made me crack. Food is important to me, and so is my digestive situation. I don't like unanticipated bathroom trips in public. I'm a grown man, but fuck, I prefer to take a shit in my own house, thank you very much.

That's what you get for suggesting she start cooking for two.

Can't take it back now. It would be a dead giveaway that her plan is working. We can't have that.

I just have no idea what I'm going to get when I come home, and I hate to admit it, but fuck, I'm nervous.

I take a deep breath and get out of my car.

I close the door quietly. You know, just in case. I don't need to warn her of my arrival. Maybe I can catch her by surprise this time.

Okay, Beck, she isn't out to get you at all times of the day. It's two in the afternoon. She's at work.

Or is she?

I'm still not fully convinced that she has a job. She leaves every single morning as if she does, but when I drove by her supposed offices the other day, the place looked vacant.

I'd ask her, but she'd just make a smart-ass comment that would get me nowhere.

Normally, I'd go through the garage, but since I'm trying this whole "don't make a sound" approach, I check to see if the door is unlocked.

It is.

Shit.

Okay, breathe. That doesn't mean anything.

It means she's home, and fuck.

Be on alert. I repeat. Be on alert.

My heart is hammering as I push the door open. Soft music is playing in the empty living room. I walk slowly, peeking into the kitchen and down the hall. Not a sign of her. I head for the basement steps but pause at the top. The lights downstairs are off.

Huh, where is she? I move for the hallway to her room, then my phone rings louder than a blow horn at a football game.

"Fuck!" I shout and hit the wall, pulling my phone from my pocket.

Calla's name is on the screen.

"Yeah?" I try to even out my breathing.

Jesus, coming home today has really shown me how much cardio I do not do. I can barely catch my breath.

"Yeah," Calla says in a mimicking tone. "Always so polite."

I don't move as I wait for her to continue—but she doesn't.

"Why are you calling me if we're both home?"

"Oh good, you're home. I was actually calling to tell you that I think I left the front door unlocked when I came home for lunch. I hope everything is okay."

"Everything is fine."

"Cool," she says in a chipper tone. "See you later."

She hangs up, and I just stand there.

I can't believe her. Making me paranoid to walk around my own house.

This is the game she wants to play, huh? Fine. Two can play, and I guarantee, I will not be the one to break.

CHAPTER FOURTEEN

CALLA

Containing my laughter is easy.

"That poor man," Greer says and stabs at her salad.

I do the same, devouring my late lunch and setting my phone down. Sabotage sure makes a girl hungry.

"He's fine. Trust me."

She looks out my passenger window and shakes her head. "I can't lie and say watching him tiptoe into the house just now and peek around as if he was about to be caught doing something bad wasn't entertaining. You must be doing something right. Do you really think he's about to cave?"

"Oh, he has to be," I say around a mouthful of lettuce, thinking of his scowl this morning when he came to the kitchen with blue hair. He had no comment, which I think said volumes. "He can't go on like this forever."

"Yeah, but he cooks for you, buys you flowers, he watches your favorite movies with you, and he—"

"He can only do that for so long, Greer. He's about to show his true colors. I can feel it."

I'm not so sure who I'm trying to convince at this point. Beck is a nice guy. Too nice. He's so laid-back and easy to be around that yes, I do feel bad about the choices I've been making. But at the end of each day, my goal hasn't changed. I need him to ask me for a divorce.

"If he didn't freak out about dying his hair blue or about the fact you spent two thousand dollars on his credit card," she pins me with a hard glare and looks in my back seat, "I'm not so sure you're right."

"Hey, I told you, I kept the receipts and went to a store that had a ninety-day return policy. He'll get his money back as soon as he files for divorce."

Still, Greer keeps shaking her head. "I don't know. I think he likes you."

"He's attracted to me. There is a big difference. As far as *like* like, he doesn't—trust me. He's just being stubborn."

"Oh, right, *he's* being stubborn."

"Yes, *he* is."

I know she thinks I'm the one who is being unreasonable here, but to be fair, I'm not alone. We are equally trying to get the other to cave. Okay, so Beck isn't actively doing anything. But, and this is a giant but, I find it hard to believe that he actually likes the way I moved the living room around, the pillows and blankets I added, the way I rearranged all his pictures on the walls, or that he truly believes the way I reorganized the house does, in fact, have a better flow. I swear he used that exact wording just to annoy me.

Which, to me, is his way of getting under my skin.

I hate to admit it, but it's working.

"I need to up my game."

"Wasn't that the point of moving things around, shopping, and coloring his hair?"

"Yes, but I need more."

"I think you need to focus on getting a real job."

I nod. "True, but this is a top priority also."

"What if," Greer says slowly, "you just started to ignore him? Go back to avoiding him, and maybe when he sees life without you around goes on, he'll be like 'Oh yeah, I never see her. We may as well part ways.'"

I tap my chin with the end of my fork.

"Interesting view."

I'm not lying when I say it, but a small part of me panics at the thought of not seeing him.

Of not waking up to him on his computer in the kitchen only to find him later in the living room and in his office at night. I want to ask him so badly why he moves around, but that would imply that I care.

"Or you could go the complete opposite route and drive him nuts with your body till he caves. Show him the goods without actually being naked and maybe tell him he can have it if he files."

"Whoa, that is smutty."

"I know. I've been reading too much lately."

"Whose books?"

Her cheeks blush. "Oh, um, just the group's. Now that I'm a new member of the… friends... I thought... I should support them all. You know."

I pull my gaze from the house to really observe my friend. She starts to pick at her salad, but her hands are shaking.

"Is everything okay?"

"Oh yeah, why?"

I tilt my head and smile.

"Are you crushing on someone from the group? Is it Tobias? No, it's Graham, isn't it? God, he's so quiet, but I could see it. I totally could."

"No, I'm not crushing on anyone from the group."

"Hmm, well, I'll have to take your word for it. Tobias is totally in love with Natalie, and Graham is probably too quiet for you, and that leaves my brother who—" I laugh before I can even think of what to say. "Is my brother. I can't even think about it."

Honestly, my brother is great. I just can't think of him dating again because—movement catches my eyes.

"Oh, he's on the move!" Greer says quickly, snapping the lid onto her salad.

I cheer and hand her my salad box. "Should we follow him?"

Greer laughs. "I really want to, but *I* still have a job and I want to keep it, so you should probably take me back soon."

"You're right. I'm sorry."

I wait until Beck is down the street, and then I turn on my car and head downtown.

"It is cool if I hang out for a bit?" I ask.

Greer is right. I really need to get a job. I can't keep hanging out with them. The last two weeks have been fun-ish, but I do need to figure things out.

"Of course. Willa and I love having you around. Every-thing is so clean when you're there."

"Enough to put me on payroll?" I tease.

"I wish."

"Me too."

As soon as I pull up in front of Willa's studio, Greer

excuses herself to walk to the post office, so I head inside and instantly spot the new decor on her walls.

"You should switch those pictures," I say. Willa is reading something on her iPad. "That way, as people walk in and when they leave, they have a motivational quote."

She lowers her device and smiles at me. "So, what you're really saying is that I should have let you decorate this place when I moved in."

I laugh. "No, it just occurred to me."

"Uh, huh. The same way the position of my desk lets me view the street just perfectly, but the sunrise and sunset won't cast a glare on my computer screen at any time of day. Or the way the weights are set up, or the way the mirror is placed to avoid bad lighting, or the way—"

"I like to stage things, okay. Is that a bad thing?"

"Nope. Not at all. In fact, I think you should start your own business."

"Doing what?" I ask. "Going house to house and telling people how I think they should change the way they decorate their living rooms or organize their kitchens?"

"Maybe, yeah. You should start your own staging and organizing businesses. Realtors would love it."

She goes back to focusing on whatever is on her iPad while I process her suggestion. I've been moving things around Beck's house in an attempt to annoy him, but all he's done is compliment where I put things or mention how something looks better in one spot than where he had it.

Coincidence?

Maybe they aren't wrong. I do enjoy doing these types of things, but could I actually make a business out of it?

"Yeah, I don't know," I answer honestly. "Everyone

knows that I'm not very good at finding something and sticking to it."

"Well, maybe that's because you haven't found what you truly want."

Could that be it?

The idea of starting my business both excites me and terrifies me. Willa might see something in me, but it's been a long time since I've been dedicated enough to something to see it through. But maybe, as she said, once I find something that truly matters to me, I'll commit and stop giving up.

"Speaking of what you truly want," Willa smiles over her screen, "how's Operation Get Beck to Divorce Me going?"

I smile but cut it off quickly. "It's not going. He likes everything I do. It's annoying. I think he's doing it on purpose."

What's even more annoying is the fact that some nights, when we're getting along and watching TV, I let myself think for a fleeting moment there could actually be something between us. It's so dumb, because it was one night in Vegas that started all this, but it was a good night for us. What if every night was like that? What if I could be that happy all the time?

"Can I ask you a question?" Willa pauses to give me a stern look. "It's a serious one."

"O-kay."

"Do you think maybe, just maybe, you like being married to Beck?"

"What?" I squeak out.

"It's just," she pauses, "being married is a big thing. It's huge. If it was wrong, no amount of proving yourself would keep someone married. They'd just get a divorce. So what if, in the back of your mind, you want to be married?"

"To Beck?"

She nods and grins.

I start to object, but her question has triggered something in my brain. Do I like it? Perhaps she—

"Your brother is coming!" Greer says, dashing through the door. "He's right—"

"Jesus, Greer, I would have walked with you. Are you okay?" my brother says, walking into Willa's studio. It's two thirty in the afternoon on a Wednesday. In his mind, I should be working.

Shit. What should I do? Just tell him the truth? If I tell him the truth, he'll most likely mention it to Beck, who will then know I've been sneaking out of the house every single day pretending I have a job. He doesn't need to know that. I'm too far in to admit I've been lying. My brother—eh, I think I've moved past the whole his opinion matters most to me phase. He'll love me either way, but Beck? I don't want him to think —shit.

My two friends are looking at me like a deer in headlights, probably wondering how I'm going to get out of this one, but my mind has shifted to the realization that Beck's opinion matters to me.

I don't want him to see me as a failure, and knowing that I care what he thinks is…

"I have to go," I blurt out and grab my purse.

"Wait, are you on your lunch hour?" Simon asks.

I pause. "Yep, late, late lunch, but I need to run an errand before it's over. I'll see you all later."

I'm out of the door before anyone can reply, but that doesn't stop Willa and Greer from texting me within minutes.

Greer: I tried to stall him.
Willa: I don't think this was about her brother. What just happened?
Greer: What else would it be over? Duh. Her husband.
Willa: I think our girl is catching feelings.
Calla: No, that's not it.

But it is. I totally am.

Greer: I think Willa is on to something.
Willa: Your brother and my client are demanding we start his appointment. I don't think he has a clue.
Greer: Remind us again why you can't just be with Beck. What's the big issue?

The issue is simple. I let myself live in a world where I was going to get everything I wanted once. Where I woke up thinking about the dream life I was going to have with the all-American family and the white picket fence. Wrong. It back-fired. It ruined me. It changed me. I'm not letting it happen again.

CHAPTER FIFTEEN
BECK

The way I see it, I have two options when it comes to Calla. One, I can have a full-blown adult conversation with her and address what she's been doing, and we can move past it. Two, I can play the game with her.

I spent a good hour weighing the pros and cons of each option and in the end, option B was more fun and seemed fitting. If Calla wanted to come to me about this and have an actual conversation, one that involves more than her begging me to file, she would have. Knowing her, if I go with the first, she'd deflect, and that would leave me with option two. I'm just skipping a pointless conversation and getting right to it.

I hear Calla's car pull into the drive, so I make myself comfortable and wait.

I'm all in now. May as well go big right out of the gate.

"Honey, I'm home," Calla calls out as she stomps through the door, singing her next line. "I went shopping."

I take a deep breath and move from the kitchen to the

living room. The smile on her face drops. As do the bags in her hands.

"Shopping, huh? What did you buy?" I move closer. Her lavender honey scent surrounds me, and I swear, no matter what this woman has done to us in the last couple of weeks, just being near her gets a rise from every part of me.

But right now, it looks like I've switched the roles, and I won't lie: the flushed look on her cheeks is worth it.

She steps back, her gaze bouncing around the room like a pinball machine.

I hold my composure and brush my arms against hers as I reach for one of the bags. She jerks her hand back like I burned her, and I almost break into laughter.

"Where is your shirt?" she asks.

"In the wash."

"All of them?"

"The ones I wanted to wear, yeah."

"And your pants are in there with them?"

I shake my head but don't look at her. I try to peek into a bag instead.

"Nope. Just haven't put them back on yet."

Finally, I look up and grin. "I'm not naked, Calla. I have my boxers on."

Her nod has a slight wobble.

Do not laugh. Do not laugh.

"Oh, wow-o, was that the dryer?" she says and moves past me. "Let's go get you some clothes."

"I'm good. What is this?" I ask, pulling a weirdly shaped object from the bag. At first glance, it looks like it could be a cross between a dog toy and a sex toy.

I hold it up for Calla.

Her eyes widen as if she's just seeing it for the first time. "You roll it against sore muscles."

Ah, okay.

"Huh, I thought maybe you had a kink I wasn't aware of."

Her bottom lip drops open.

I move toward her slowly, toy in hand, and gently touch it to her chin to close her mouth. "Too bad."

Her chest rises with her next breath. I lick my lips and glance at hers.

"I went shopping," she says again and shoves the bags at me. "Let me show you what else I bought." She dashes right back out the door. "I'll get the rest!"

I'm smiling at my handiwork when my phone rings from the kitchen table.

Doug. I cringe. He isn't going to like anything I have to say because I'm not going to say anything he wants to hear.

"Hey, Doug, how's it going?"

"Beck! Oh my god, you are a genius."

"I am?"

I turn back around as Calla comes in with more bags and runs back out.

Hell, what did she buy?

I step closer to the bags.

"Oh, here's your card." She pops back inside and tosses my credit card at me.

How the hell did she get this?

"This book is your best work yet. I want more. Get me more."

Only being able to focus on one issue at a time, I close my eyes and focus on Doug.

"What book are we talking about?"

"The whole enemies slash roommates to lovers who accidentally got married thing. I want that. Flesh it out and get it to me. The whole book. Netflix loves the pitch I gave them."

The enemies slash roommates to—oh fuck. Fuck. Fuck. A hot tingle runs through my blood.

"Whoa, whoa, whoa," I say and jog to the stairs and down to my office.

I drop into my chair and wiggle my mouse to wake up my laptop. How the hell does he know about that?

Shit.

"Did I send that to you?" I ask. "If I did, I didn't mean to."

"No, you didn't. Remember when you shared your last pitch on Google Drive?"

Ohhh fuck. I deleted the words in the document when he said they were shit, and then I started this in the same file. Fuck.

"Right, well," I navigate to the document to change the share settings, "that's not my next book. It's just something fun to work on to clear my mind."

"Too late. I cleaned up the first few chapters and sent them to Netflix. They want it. HBO is even fighting for it to make a ten-episode mini-series. They offered to double your advance for it."

Double.

Hell, that's good money.

Really good money.

"Holy shit, are you serious?"

I didn't use my name or Calla's, so no one knows it's us. And the heroine isn't the brother's little sister in my book. I was only writing our situation out because, yeah, it's comical, but writing something that doesn't require me to think too hard was therapeutic. I did it to remind my mind of how to craft a story.

No one would know.

Except me… and Calla.

The excitement dissolves.

"It's not my next book," I tell him again.

I could never do that to Calla. Plus, she's not an idiot. Once the book was released, she'd know. Then again, she doesn't read my books… but no, I'm not doing it. I'm trying to gain her trust, albeit in a twisted way, but nonetheless, I am. This would not help our situation.

"Beck, if we don't use this book, you have one week to get me a new idea. One as good as this one. No, scratch that. One that is better. If I don't hear from you by next Friday, I'm giving the highest bidder the go-ahead to contract this."

The urge to yell "I said no!" into the phone is strong, but hell, he's right. I need a book. This will just serve as motivation to brainstorm harder.

"Give me two weeks."

He sighs through the speaker. "Two weeks it is. If we don't have a story, this publisher can and *will* pull this five-book deal you signed with them last year, and both producers will more than likely blacklist your name."

Fuck.

I pinch the spot between my eyes.

"You don't have to remind me."

"Maybe I do, and maybe you should step back on the self-publishing side to focus on this."

"Well, maybe they should take all my ideas. I wouldn't need to self-publish in that case."

"Whoa," Doug replies to my snappy tone. "Okay, let's

step back. Is something going on in your life that's stalling your writing?"

"No," I answer quickly. "Nothing is going on in my life."

"Well, we've never been in a situation like this. In the past, you'd jump on this offer."

"Yeah, I know. I just…"

I can't tell him the truth. I don't even know what it is anymore.

"I'll get you something."

"Good."

"And Doug," I speak up before he can hang up.

"Yeah?"

"Netflix and HBO." I let out a laugh of disbelief. "Wow."

"Exactly. Figure it out. Let me know."

"Thanks."

We hang up, and a chill runs over me. I'm standing in my office in my underwear. My chin drips to my chest. I have lost all control in my life.

Hell.

I walk into the laundry room, pull a shirt and sweatpants from the drying rack, and put them on. The dryer light is blinking, so the load is done and there are clothes to be folded. I open it, only to slam it shut when I see the pile of clothes inside.

I cannot fold her clothes right now. Panties and short shorts are not what my mind needs to look at right now. No. All I need to focus on is a computer screen.

Sooner rather than later.

My career depends on it.

I step out of the laundry room but pause when the dryer starts to fluff again.

Fuck it.

I'll just fold these clothes first.

Then my mind will be clear.

CHAPTER SIXTEEN

BECK

I'm never sleeping again.

My fingers whizz over the keyboard as I get out every last detail of last night's dream.

"Don't stop. Don't ever stop."

Even if I can catch my breath, I won't.

"Do that again, Beck. Again!"

My hips jerked faster and faster as I hold onto her.

"Yes!" her sweet voice calls out, the sound provoking my pending orgasm as it shoots down my spine and through my body.

"Fuck me!" I growl, shooting all I have inside her. The smile on her lips causes the sensation to linger, the sated expression on her face making me realize I'm too far gone for the woman underneath me.

· · ·

I delete the words as soon as I'm done.

Lesson learned, but motherfucker.

I should have known folding Calla's clothes and seeing her thongs *again*—if folding is even what you'd call it—was going to be a trigger for me. Yeah, I paused too many times to count, imagining her in these tiny pieces of fabric, but I didn't think that was enough to fill my nights with sex dreams.

I haven't woken up with an erection that hard since I was in junior high. It was the first night I'd spent the night at Simon's. We'd spent the afternoon at the pool, and fucking hell, Calla was the star of that dream too.

Have I been a fool for her since I was a kid and never knew it till I married her?

I head into the kitchen, the house eerily silent.

Living with Calla has been… enlightening.

I'm just putting the last dish in the dishwasher when she comes upstairs, dressed and ready for the day. She's wearing a pair of dress pants and a light pink blouse that I can see through. I think it's made that way but fuck me if the outline of her bra under that shirt doesn't send my mind to places it shouldn't go.

I'm never sleeping again.

"Good morning," she says with a big smile. "Oh, shoot balls, did I leave dishes in the sink again?"

I look down at the now-empty sink and then back at her with a smile. I'm guessing this is one of the many things on her list she's been doing to get under my skin.

"You did, but lucky for you, I actually enjoy doing the dishes. It's like a calming way for my brain to fix something without having to put much work into it. Leaves me more room to be creative with my writing."

Her smile drops. "You like doing the dishes?"

"I do."

I open the cabinet for my cereal, but it's not there. I close that cabinet and go for another.

"Everything okay?" Calla asks.

"Yeah." I rub the back of my neck. She wouldn't move my food around, would she? That would be… an odd thing to do. "I just thought I had some cereal in here, but I guess I'm out. Need anything from the store?"

"No, thank you. And you weren't out. I was rearranging the cabinets and noticed how much sugar was in those boxes and tossed them."

I stare at her. She's smiling like she did me a favor, but I have a routine, and that cereal is part of my routine.

Don't freak out. It's just food. Just take an energy drink and head to your office. She's doing this on purpose. Don't play into it.

"Thank you," I manage to say while mentally reminding myself to hide the goods when I get back from the store later.

"Of course."

I jerk the fridge open and pause again.

"Oh yes, do you know how high the chances of heart problems are from drinking energy drinks? Huge. I tossed those too. I'll see you after work. Have a good day," she says with a cheery voice and walks out the front door.

I don't have a chance to dwell on it before my phone rings.

"Hello?" I answer without looking at the name on the screen.

"Hey, I'm glad I caught you," Doug says. I can hear his music in the background and a horn honking.

"Are you talking in the car again? You know you're a shit driver when you talk and drive."

I head down to my office without food and without a drink.

Oddly enough, this has inspired me to write.

"I just pulled over."

Another horn honks, and he groans.

"Fine. Fine. I'm pulling over now."

I laugh and lean back in my seat. Honestly, with the lack of ideas I've sent him recently, I expected this call a lot sooner.

"What's up, Doug?"

"What's up? *What's up?* HBO just sent in a new offer. I'm forwarding it to you now."

I refresh my email and then suck in a breath at the zeros on the screen.

"Is this real?" I ask.

"Completely. Now, I don't want to pressure you, but this —this is once in a lifetime. I just wanted to make sure you saw it asap. Call me later, after you've had time to process it."

He hangs up.

Fuck.

Could I release a book based on my life, let it be turned into a movie, and still win over the girl who happens to also be part of that book?

I dial the only person who might have time to listen to my problems right now.

"Beck, hey, what's up?"

"Can I come over?"

Graham laughs. "Right now?"

"Yeah. It's a book and personal issue. I need help."

"A personal issue. You? Heck yeah, come over. This is new for me."

"I'm on my way," I say and rush out to my car.

I stop by Love's A Brewing for a couple of coffees, but I don't see my sister or future brother-in-law who owns the place, so I'm quickly back on my way to Graham's.

He's waiting at the door for me.

"Let's talk about your personal problem, because I'll be honest, I thought you had a perfect life. Knowing you don't brings me an odd sense of peace."

"Glad I could help and—are you moving again?" I ask, spotting the unpacked boxes.

"Oh, no, I just haven't unpacked yet."

"I know I'm here to talk out my problems, but maybe we should talk about yours. You moved in at the beginning of the summer. Two months before I bought my house. I'm fully unpacked."

He shakes his head. "Like I said, I thought you were too perfect."

I set my computer bag down.

"I wrote a book a little too close to my personal life and Doug got a hold of it and now Netflix and HBO want it, but it's… personal. If I can't give Doug something else, I'm going to lose this joint book/movie deal, and it's massive. We're talking about never having to worry about plane ticket prices again or pay off my house kind of massive. I'm not so sure I can pass it up."

"Damn," Graham says and lets out a long breath. "You should be a little more vague so I can totally not help you out."

I grab a glass from his cabinet and fill it with water from the fridge.

"Oh, I married Calla in Vegas, and I have no idea how to get her to fall for me, and that's what the book is about. Me and her. Our situation. It's basically us without our real names."

He doesn't say anything right away, and I look up.

His eyes are wide, and his mouth is hanging open. I wave my hand in front of his face, and he jerks back.

"What?"

"Oh, you heard me."

"You married Simon's sister?" he asks.

I take a seat at his table and pull out my computer. His MacBook is already set up. Maybe I can convince him to do some sprints with me. Sometimes that helps. Maybe a new idea will spark.

"Yep."

"You married your best friend's sister."

I glance up. "Yes."

"You married Calla Stone?"

"You know, no matter how you phrase it, the answer is still yes."

He joins me at the table.

"Are you insane? I mean, what the hell were you two thinking? How drunk were you? Does Simon know? Who all knows? Oh god, is this why she moved in with you?"

"Whoa," I hold my hands up. "Slow down. You're the first person I've told. I don't know who she has told, but neither of us have told Simon. That I'm sure of. Wow. It feels good to say that out loud." I blow out a breath. "Okay, this book deal is—"

"Hold on," Graham cuts me off. "I fully want to get into the fact that HBO wants your books, because holy shit, but I need more details. Are you into her? I thought you two hated each other."

"We do. Did. I don't know."

"Well, one night you liked each other enough to get married."

It was a good night. One of my best.

I nod. "Yeah, I like her. It's weird, because she makes it clear as day that she doesn't care for me, but that night in Vegas…" I shake my head. "I can't get that woman out of my mind, and even now, I see glimpses of her and I just… I don't know how to get her attention romantically. Which is honestly just crazy because all she does is drive me insane. All these games she plays. It should make me not like her, right? Instead, it just makes me more curious about her. Like I'm seeing this new creative side of her that I never got to see before, and I'm into it. Hell, it makes me want to play games too."

"I get it." Graham cuts me off. "The more you live with her and the more you get to know, you like her more. So, yes, okay, what have you tried romantically to get her attention?"

"What do you mean?"

"What have you done to flirt or ask her out or what?"

I sit up taller. "Huh."

"What?" His eyes light up. "What have you done?"

"Nothing. I haven't done anything. Just flowers a few times. I cook, I clean. I guess I hoped that by being married and living together, it would just happen."

His face scrunches up like he smells something rotten. "No wonder she hasn't fallen for you. Now, while those are great qualities to have in a husband, you need to put in more effort. Hers might be to annoy the living hell out of you, but at least she's trying something. What does she like?"

"Honestly, I'm not sure. One moment I think I know her and the next, I don't."

"Start small then. Cook her dinner. She works all day, right?"

"I've done that before, but I could make it more special." I point a finger at him. "You might be onto something."

"Of course I am. Now, let's talk about this movie deal and this book."

I groan. We spend the next two hours listing new plot ideas.

None of them stick though because all I can think about is how to create the most romantic dinner for Calla.

Tonight's the night she starts to fall for me.

CHAPTER SEVENTEEN
CALLA

I'm not dealing with a typical man.

Beck is one of a kind, and I need to look at this from a different perspective.

But how?

Hell, I have no idea what I'm doing.

And now that he walks around half naked, I'm way out of my league here.

I let my mind think on it for another few minutes, but nothing comes up, so I grab my laptop.

I shouldn't be thinking of Beck anyway. I should be looking for a new job. I would probably have one by now if I hadn't been putting so much time and effort into this whole Beck thing.

I mean, if this whole sabotage thing works and I end up moving out, how will I even pay for my own place if I don't have a job? *Ha, ha, what place, Calla? You don't have that either.*

Clearly, I don't need to worry because I'm not even good at sabotage.

I spend twenty minutes searching for a job but find nothing.

Beck likes doing dishes to clear his mind. What do I like to do that clears my mind? What's something I like to do that I just enjoy without having to put much thought into it?

Organizing is the only thing I can think of.

Ooh!

I jump from the bed.

I'm going to reorganize his entire kitchen so he can't find a single thing. The food was purely because his cabinets were a mess, but this—this could be good.

He's closed off in his office right now, so this is as good a time as any. It's like a win-win: I get to do something I enjoy and annoy him at the same time.

It's genius.

I sneak upstairs and, cabinet by cabinet, plate by plate, bowl by bowl, macaroni box by macaroni box—I move every last thing this kitchen has to offer. I even move the steaks he clearly took out for dinner back to the freezer and throw the candles that still had tags on them and some lavender bubbles to a hidden drawer by the back door. Whoever he was planning to wine and dine tonight with those babies, well, surprise. Good luck to you on another night. Not only am I smiling at my handiwork a couple hours later, but I'm happily back in my room, snuggled in with a book.

Whack.

Whack.

Whack.

I whip the cover off my body and march to Beck's office. I choose not to knock before I go inside because hell, he clearly doesn't care about courtesy with my wall and his stupid ball, so why should I care about him in his office?

I swing the door open, and he turns, clearly startled. The ball bounces off the wall and hits him on the side of the head. Just like the last time.

Good.

I nod, satisfied with that small detail, and retreat to my room.

"Are you serious right now?" Beck growls and judging by the volume, he's following me. "You can't just come into my office like that."

"Yes, I can."

"No, you can't."

I pause in my doorway and spin around. My hand is in the air ready to poke him, but the small fact that he's shirtless seems to have snuck by me while I was in his doorway.

My eyes fall like magnets to his chiseled chest, to his sculpted arms, to the abs that have haunted my dreams the last few nights.

I slowly drag my gaze back up, and a cocky smirk greets me.

"Want me to step back so you can get a better look?"

Damn it.

I roll my eyes and shake my head. "Stop tossing that ball against my wall. There are three others for you to choose from."

He nods, having the audacity to look a little guilty. "Sorry. I'm not used to someone being in that room when I'm in a block." He turns to head back to his office. "I'll hit a different wall."

"Wait," I call out and inwardly cringe. Why am I stopping him? Why do I want to ask him about his books?

Oh, maybe because you've been secretly binge reading all his books and want to know which one is next.

"You're blocked? Like on a book?"

He nods. "Yep."

"Which book?"

He crosses his arms and leans in his doorway. "That's the block. I need a new one, and it seems I'm out of ideas."

I snort. "Unlikely."

He shrugs.

"Seriously?"

A nod.

"I thought you guys were all inspired constantly."

"Sadly, we are not."

"Do you know why?"

"Why are you so curious?"

I shake my head and look at the floor. "I'm not."

"Right."

He knocks on the doorframe and then disappears. I don't hear the click of his door, however, so I groan quietly and follow him.

"Okay, I'm a little curious. What do you do if you can't write?"

He tosses the ball at me. I barely catch it before it beans me in the eye.

"Oh, yes, the magic ball."

He lets out a huff of a laugh. "If only."

I set the ball down on his desk. "Maybe I can help."

I regret the offer as soon as it is out of my mouth. Not in a "I don't want to help him" way, but in a "why am I subjecting myself to more time with him when my end goal is the exact opposite?"

Oh, right, because at the end of the day, no matter how I treat him, he's still a human and well, the stiffness in his shoulders and his lack of banter has me all off kilter. And I can't believe I'm admitting this, but he's not terrible to be around.

"You want to help me?"

"I could try."

"Have you ever written a book?"

I shake my head. "Obviously not, but I've read plenty. Where do we start?"

"It's really okay, Calla. Thank you for offering, but I'll figure this out. I always do. I just need to determine what this block is and why I can't think of a good love story. Hell, I can't even think of a steamy scene, and those are usually my go-to chapters when I'm stuck. I write the sex scenes first to find out what kind of characters I have. That's where I see what they really—wow, okay, I have no idea why I'm telling you this."

"Tell me more," I say and sit in the chair across from him, hugging my knees to my chest. "Talk it out."

He rubs a hand over his chin as a smile touches his lips.

"Just try it," I encouraged him. "What can it hurt? Tell me why you can't write a sex scene."

His eyes close, and he shakes his head.

"Boy, you really lost all your words, didn't you?"

"Seems that way."

He finally looks at me, but his gaze flickers to my chest so fast I almost miss it. He starts to blush.

I glance down to see that my nipples are on high alert through my T-shirt. I cross my arms quickly.

Shit.

"Sorry, I shouldn't have looked."

I open my mouth to say something snarky, but I change course quickly. He thinks he gets to do this to me. Nope. No way.

I stand and smile.

"Writing about sex should be no problem now. Just write about my round, perky breasts. Seems you've got the image of them fresh in your mind." With that, I turn and walk out of his office. "I'll just be upstairs eating dinner," I shout behind me. "If you need more inspiration."

Beck comes rushing out of the office.

"What?" I turned around quickly. "What's wrong?"

"I'm going to cook you dinner. I'm grilling rib eyes. I even got you some things to relax with while I cook," he says with a proud grin and walks right by me and up the stairs, skipping them two at a time.

Umm, what just happened?

Oh shit, the bubbles and candles were for me.

I close my eyes, cringing as I picture what he's about to find.

Damn, a hot bath with flickering candles sounds really nice too.

Slowly, I make my way to the kitchen to find him standing in front of the cabinet where his plates used to be.

I'm unsure of what to say, and I feel a little guilty for

evidently impacting his writing time with my nonsense of intentionally annoying him when he so clearly planned something sweet for me.

He starts laughing so hard that he folds over.

My lips tug into a smile, but I'm not sure if I should laugh with him or be scared he might be going insane.

"I… I have no idea where anything is," he finally says. "It's my kitchen, and I'm lost."

"Yeah, I, um, I just thought the flow of where things went was better this way."

His gaze jerks to mine, and I expect him to say something snappy, but he doesn't.

"Grab your coat. I'm taking you out."

"Oh yeah, you know." I wave my hand to dismiss his offer. "I'm busy and—"

"Get your coat, Calla." His deep voice makes my nipples stand at attention.

He notices and smiles. "Maybe a sweater too."

"I'm not sure what's happening here, but I'm confused."

"We can talk about it at dinner."

"Really, Beck."

"Calla. Coat. Now. Let's go."

I narrow my gaze at him. "I want tacos."

"Fine."

"And a margarita."

"Good."

At this point, he's retrieved my coat from the coat closet, and he tosses it at me.

"Ready?"

"You're driving."

"Yes, I am."

And with that, he opens the front door and the car door for and takes me to my favorite Mexican restaurant.

I sigh.

Damn it. I'm closer to dating my husband than divorcing him.

This is not part of the plan.

Tonight, I will eat good food. Tomorrow, I will create a new plan.

CHAPTER EIGHTEEN
BECK

Just write about my round, perky breasts.

Hell, I haven't been able to think about anything since. And that was after only looking at them through her shirt. The first time I said the word *sex*, they stood at attention. I can't believe she didn't notice me looking more than once.

I felt like a fucking teenager who just saw his first nipple.

I shake my head, focusing on the road as I drive us to dinner, but I can't seem to clear our earlier conversation.

Why can't you write a sex scene?

Oh, you know, because when I do, all I think about are the things I want to do to her and how I can't, so I wrote them down because the building pressure is fucking torture.

Not that I am going to tell her all that.

She's built me up in her mind as this villain she can never be friends with, let alone something more. Which is crazy because we have chemistry. Fighting or not, the energy between us is electric. How does she not see that? Hell, how does she not feel it?

I pull into the parking lot and push the ignition off.

"Should we just order it to go?" she asks before reaching for the handle.

"No, why would we do that?"

She twists to face me. "Because this is weird, isn't it?"

"Dinner?"

"Us. Eating dinner together. Out. Like we are on a date."

I nod my head a little. "Yeah, it is a little out of the ordinary for us. I won't lie there, but come on, Calla. Nothing about our situation is normal. Every day is about going with the flow, and right now, the flow is eating dinner. A big fat taco and lots and lots of chips."

She presses her lips together to hold back her smile.

I want to reach over and brush my hand to her cheek and tell her she can relax with me, that it's okay to be happy around me, but she jumps out before I get the chance.

I follow her, a crisp mid-September breeze brushing her hair over her shoulder. She grips the front of her jacket tighter around her body.

I open the door to the restaurant, and she steps inside. My stomach rumbles at the smell of freshly baked chips.

"Wow, you really are hungry."

"Famished."

I hold two fingers up to the waitress. She smiles in return. I've been here enough times to know that half the staff doesn't speak English, but they are some of the most polite people I've ever met.

She shows us to a booth, and Calla and I take separate sides.

Water and chips and salsa are set in front of us immediately, and neither of us waste time digging in.

"Did you not eat today because you were working on your book?" Calla asks.

I let out a sigh.

"Attempting to write one, yes."

I'd fill her in on my issue, but I don't want to ruin the night. I still don't even know if I'm going to say yes to Doug. But fuck, I don't think I have a choice unless I want to say goodbye to my reputation.

"Does this happen often?"

"No." I shake my head. "Normally, I can solve a wonky plot pretty fast, but I've been a little distracted."

"I wonder why," she says, looking past me and sipping her water.

"Yeah, I wonder."

Her gaze flicks briefly to mine. I wish she let me look into her eyes longer, but this is Calla. I'm fascinated with a woman who likes to keep me on her toes. Perhaps I need to remind her that the two of us know each other a lot better than we think.

"Let me guess," I say as she sets her menu down. "You're going to get the steak fajita salad without the tortilla shell, extra lettuce, and light on the peppers."

Shit. I do know her.

I chuckle as her bottom lip drops.

"How do you know that?"

"I've known you since we were kids, Calla. I pay attention. Twenty bucks says you won't be able to guess my order, though."

She rolls her eyes.

"Smothered chicken burrito with extra cheese and green chili on the side."

Damn.

"Huh, and here I thought you hated me enough to not notice something as simple as my order at a Mexican restaurant."

Her left brow rises with her smile, but she doesn't say anything. Our waiter comes, we place our orders, adding a margarita on the rocks for each of us.

Since we've broached the topic lightly, now might be a good time to ask why specifically she doesn't care for me. If I knew, I could remedy it, and maybe even redeem myself. Fix one problem, then maybe the next would follow.

"So, I have to ask—"

"Oh my god. Oh my god. Oh my god." Calla jumps from her side of the booth, rushing to mine and pushing me farther into the booth so she can sit by me.

She twists to face me with a hand blocking one side of her face.

"Everything okay?" I ask.

"My brother just walked in with Grey."

"Really?" I start to rise, but she pulls me back down.

"Don't."

"They could join us."

"No, they can't."

I chuckle. "Why not?"

Her head tilts, and she glares at me.

Ah. She doesn't want him to see us together.

"Let me see where he's sitting."

I slowly rise to peek over the booth but drop quickly.

"He's coming this way."

"Shit. Shit. Please don't let him see us. It'll come with questions, and I hate lying to him, and I—"

I can let her keep ranting and chance her brother hearing her voice, or I can do something to definitely make sure he doesn't see us as the waiter walks past our table to seat him.

Option B is the obvious choice, as I've learned, if I want to get on her good side. My insta plan though—maybe not.

I grab her face and crush my lips to hers; all panic in her voice quickly comes to a halt. I run a hand through her hair and pull her closer. The placement of my arm and hand should shield our faces long enough for him to pass by without noticing us. When I think enough time has passed, I pull back, but the slip of her tongue past my lips brings me back. She moans and then jerks away.

Her eyes are wide, and she sucks in a breath.

"That was, um, a great idea. Thank you."

She touches her lips, and I chuckle.

"You're welcome."

She faces the table and then practically jumps into my lap.

"I can see him from where I'm sitting. We need to move to the other side."

"Why don't we just tell him we came here for dinner because you rearranged my kitchen—which, by the way, even though I have no idea where to find anything, it looks amazing. You should be a professional organizer—and I didn't have the patience to find everything to cook a meal. It's the truth."

We lock gazes, and for a moment I think she's going to agree.

"Not tonight. Please, Beck."

Something in her voice tugs at my heart, so I nod.

"How do we get to the other side?"

"Crawl under the table," she answers, as if it's the only option.

Our food shows up at that moment.

"Can you box this up for us?" I ask. The waiter nods and then comes right back to the table with boxes and the check.

"Are we sneaking out?" Calla asks.

"Beats crawling on the floor," I say, putting cash in the ticket book. "What's he doing now?"

"Good point." She peeks around the booth. "He's turned around talking to the table behind him."

"Good. Go."

We dash out, climbing into my SUV. I'm just about to back out when Calla's hand latches onto my wrist.

"Look," she gasps and points out the front window. "That's Greer."

"Popular place tonight."

"Is she meeting my brother?" Calla's face lights up.

"No clue."

"Don't you two talk?" she asks.

"Not too much since I married his sister and can't talk to him about it."

"Touché. Let's go see."

"See what?" I ask with a smile.

Her mood is playful, and I'm here for it.

"If she's meeting Simon."

"Like a spy?"

"Just like it. You need inspiration for a book, right? A little sneaking around and spying might be just what you need."

It's not typically what I write, but she might be onto something.

"Aren't we too old to do this?" I ask.

"How far are you willing to go to write this book? Please, Beck."

Like before, her pleading tugs at my heart. I've seen Calla smile more times in the last thirty minutes than she has since she moved in with me.

I nod. "Fine."

We both get out. Calla comes around the back of my car, crouched down. She grabs my hand and leads me through cars until we can see her brother's table through the window.

Sure enough, Greer sits with Simon and Grey.

Calla starts clawing at me with excitement.

"How cute is this?" She grins.

I take another look through the window at my smiling friend. Simon deserves to be happy. They could be here as friends, but either way, I can't remember the last time Simon was out with a woman who wasn't his mother or sister. And with Grey there too. This could be something, but it could also be nothing. However, Calla is beaming, and I'm not going to ruin that.

"This turned out to be a great night," she says, pushing me to go back to the car.

"Yeah?"

"Yes, and I'm with you." She pushes me. "Stop smiling at me like that. I know, I know. Don't make it a thing."

"I didn't say anything."

"You looked at me."

"How did I look at you?"

"Like this is a thing."

"What's that look like?"

"It looks like you right now, giving me a goofy grin, and me feeling… just get in the car. I'm hungry."

I do as I'm told, not pressing the subject more, because she's right. Tonight was good, and it needs to end well.

She pops open the top to the chips and salsa as I pull out of the parking lot.

A little progress is still progress, and I might have changed her mind on me a little tonight.

There might be a chance for us after all.

CHAPTER NINETEEN
CALLA

Beck is… Beck is…

This man is just like the guys he writes about in his books. He's more sweetheart with just the right amount of irresistible than I ever expected him to be.

Holy hell.

"We have a problem," I say as soon as I step through the door of Willa's studio. "A big problem."

And I'm not just talking about what I saw in his boxer briefs this morning.

Boxer briefs! I swear that man did that on purpose.

"Oh, do tell." Greer grins and greets me with a hug. "Does this have to deal with your dear husband?"

"Sure does."

I'm about to tell them everything when Nora Quinn walks in. "Good morning, am I early?"

"No, you're right on time. Calla just dropped in to share some news," Willa says and points to the chair in front of her desk.

Nora must be here for an appointment. Sooner or later, I was bound to show up when Willa had a client who wasn't my brother.

"Nora is going to help me with my company's presence online," she says, as if she knows I'm debating whether I should leave. "She might be able to help with your situation as well."

"I didn't even tell you what it is yet."

"Yeah, well, Nora is a problem-solver, and considering the advice Greer and I sent you off with last time, I'm assuming that is part of the big problem you just announced, yeah?"

I nod.

I bet she can help.

Nora, who has been looking back and forth between Willa and me, takes a seat. "Are you all about to share some girl gossip with me? Because I won't lie; I need it. I need it badly. Natalie is always out of town with Griffin, and I spend way too much time with Hero and the boys."

"Tell me about it. I love Zane, but those boys love, *love* to be together."

Nora laughs. "It's cute and annoying how much they care for each other."

"Isn't it? Sometimes I think—"

"Oh my god," I cut in and then slump against the wall. "Is this my future?" I point to Willa and Nora. "Hanging out and talking about how cute and annoying our husb—" I shut my mouth instantly. Only Greer and Willa know that Beck and I are married. "You know, I think I will come back."

Greer stops me. "She might be able to get the information you need. You know she's married to Hero and just said she spends a lot of time with the boys."

"Speaking of spending time with the boys, did you go on a date with my brother last night?" I ask Greer. Her eyes go wide, and she waves her hands in front of her.

"No, why?"

"I saw you."

"You did? Why didn't you come to say hi?"

"Um, because you two were on a date."

And I was on a date with my husband, but that's not the point of this current conversation.

"It wasn't a date. Trust me. We are just friends. Your brother is pretty cool, and I... need to stop dating altogether. Just write men off."

I study her for a moment, but the disappointed look in her eyes does it for me. I believe her.

I let out a big breath.

"Guys are so complicated, and Beck is leading the pack."

"Alright." Nora puts her hand up. "I'm invested now even though I know nothing. It sounds like something fun."

"It's really not," I reply. My gaze falls to Willa and Greer, who both nod to Nora.

I'm not saying they're wrong about me sharing with Nora; I'm just worried that the more people who find out... well, eventually it's going to get to my brother or my parents. It's not that I think they'll be disappointed. It's that if they know, they would be happy. Too happy. So happy that once Beck and do finally get divorced, it will crush them.

I let out a breath and nod. I guess that's all the more reason I need to get advice from anyone who's willing to give it.

"Beck and I got married in Vegas over the summer, and now we live together, and he won't get a divorce because he thinks we need to find out why we made a rash decision like that, and I won't get one because everyone in my life thinks I can't commit. So in order to get divorced, I need him to initiate it, and he hasn't yet. I've been doing everything in my power to annoy and bother and irritate him, but it's not working. Now almost anytime I come home, he's just casually hanging out in the house in nothing but his boxer briefs."

I close my eyes, and the image of him stalking toward me is burned into my mind. I let out a frustrated growl. "He always has fresh flowers on the table for me, and I love flowers. I didn't know it till now, but I do. I don't know what to do anymore."

"Damn," Greer says. "That is a tough problem. A hot half-naked man to come home to and he's good to you. What a shame."

"Cut the sarcasm, please. I had no idea that the little things would matter. He pays attention. This is new for me."

"You have a man at home who clearly wants you."

"No." I shake my index finger in the air. "He's up to something."

"Like you were up to something?" Willa asks, turning her computer to Nora, who is staring at me, eyes wide.

"You married Beck, and no one knows?" A smile touches her lips. "This is amazing. Three of them are married off. Well, basically." She smiles at Willa. "We all know Zane isn't going to wait much longer. This is just so cool! Think of all the parties we will have together and when we all have kids and—"

"Hello? Did you hear me? I'm trying to get Beck to end this marriage."

"Are you sure? Kind of sounds like you're into your husband."

"Or," I don't know exactly where I'm headed with this sentence, "he's up to something."

"Maybe he knows," Greer chimes in. She's washing the front window to change out the signs. "Maybe he's trying to get you to crack by getting to you the way you got to him."

"I didn't walk around naked, but you could be onto something."

"Call his bluff!"

"Yes!"

"Ha. I don't think you three are listening to me."

"We are," Greer laughs.

"Um, alright. Well, if that were true, then you'd know there is no way I could do that. I'm just going to say it right now so we're all on the same page: if that man tries to get me in bed, I'm pretty sure I'd let him take me. There is so much tension between us. My problem now is that not only do I need him to divorce me, but I also need to not want him. I need to not like that he cleans the kitchen every night or that he folds towels better than me or that—"

I need to not like anything about him. A girl with my condition is not the girl for Beck Robertson.

"Holy shit, you really, *really* like your husband," Greer squeals.

"I know!"

I cover my face with my hands and take a deep breath.

I am so absolutely screwed.

CHAPTER TWENTY

BECK

Today, I woke up with a plan. I took what Calla and I shared last night as a sign to put more effort in. To make my move. Show her how good we can be together.

Flowers are my go-to right now, and that's only because whenever I have a new bunch in the kitchen, Calla's face lights up. She tries to hide it, but I've seen. So yeah, more flowers it is.

To say I was shocked when the florist called me to say she couldn't deliver the flowers because that company doesn't exist anymore is an understatement.

If her place of employment is closed, where the hell does she go every day?

I'll tell you where. To Willa's studio. I just happened to see her in the front window when I was taking some signed books to the post office.

Could I have just gone in and asked what's up? Sure, but I felt this was more of a conversation to have in private.

I've been waiting all day for her to come home so I can ask her about it. There's clearly a reason she hasn't told me or her brother for that matter. I'm going to find out what that is.

I'm reading in the living room when Calla comes through the door from the garage.

"Hey, baby, how was work?"

Calla stiffens and slowly turns to face me.

"Good. Long."

"Busy?"

"Very."

She shrugs off her coat and puts it in the closet.

"Want to talk about it? Looks like it was a rough one, and I'd love to discuss it with you."

She keeps walking past me. "No thanks."

"Were you late?"

"No."

"Did you leave early?"

"No."

"Did you take a part-time job with Willa, or do you want to tell me what's really going on?"

She jerks to a stop and spins around.

"What was that?"

"I said, where do you actually work?"

"In a billing department," she answers without missing a beat.

"For which company?"

She cocks a hip and crosses her arms.

"I'm sorry, Daddy, was I supposed to run every choice I make through you? No. No, I was not."

A smart-ass response is stuck on my lips. She just called me Daddy.

Do I like it?

I've written about it before.

Readers love it.

Yet considering that I actually know her parents and have met her father, it doesn't sit well with me.

I don't like it.

"Oh, cat got your tongue?"

Her cackling laugh reminds me of the topic at hand and makes me smile. Calla is so expressive with her emotions, and I love it.

"See now," I say and rise from the couch, "I don't think you have a job."

She gasps loudly and covers her heart with her hand.

"And where would I go each day?"

Alright, now I don't know Calla like the back of my hand, but I know her well enough to know she's lying. There is no tell; I just know. Unless, of course, you want to call her horrible acting skills a tell.

"I cannot believe you would accuse me of such… such—"

"You don't have a job, do you?"

"I… is there a point to this conversation?"

I walked slowly toward her. She doesn't try to move even when I'm standing toe to toe with her. Her scent swallows me. Her gaze connects with mine, and she doesn't flinch.

I almost back down.

I lick my lips, and just as I thought, her eyes flicker to my mouth.

"I had to pick up those flowers from the floral shop today." I point to the bouquet of lilies on the table behind her. "Because they couldn't deliver them to you. At work. In the billing department."

"Oh" is all she says and looks at the floor.

I gently touch her chin and force her to look at me.

From the glaze in her eyes, it's clear she's on the verge of tears.

"Do you want to talk about it?" I ask.

"Not really."

"Okay." I drop my arms to my sides and rock back on my heels. "You know I'm here for you if you want to change that, right?"

"Sure," she nods.

She turns to head toward the stairs, but I reach out and stop her.

"Do you?"

"What do you want from me, Beck?"

I tilt my head and give her a look, and it must piss her off because she squares her stance to mine and puts her hands on her hips.

"You said you wanted to stay married because marriage is important to your family, and yet I haven't seen them once. You haven't mentioned them once. I can't tell if you're lying to get under my skin or if—"

"I'm not lying. I just don't see the point in bringing our families into this until we figure it out. I want to stay married to figure this out for us."

"There isn't anything to figure out, Beck."

"Do you really think there's nothing between us? You can honestly say that to me?"

She hesitates. Her lips part, but she heads for the stairs instead.

I'm right behind her.

"Calla, don't run off this time. Talk to me."

She stops at the top of the stairs but doesn't look at me.

"I'm sorry." And just like the last time she said those words to me, my heart sinks.

If I can't find a way to get through to her, there's no way I'll be able to keep her.

CHAPTER TWENTY-ONE
CALLA - VEGAS

"Holy shit, we're married," I say, tucked under Beck's arm. He kisses the top of my head and then spins me and presses me against the wall. He cups my ass and lifts me to wrap my legs around him.

His lips are on my neck, then my chest.

"Let's go to your room," I tell him.

"My thoughts exactly."

He lets me down and clasps his hand in mine as we head for the elevators.

"When should we tell Simon?" he asks.

"Definitely tomorrow. He's probably asleep, and I don't want to wake him or Grey right now."

"Oh my gosh," Beck says and stops. "I'm an uncle now."

I laugh. "Technically, yes."

He chuckles and tugs me along. Giddy, I latch onto his arms and walk beside him. I'm a married woman, and I'm not scared about it one little bit.

"This is just so crazy. I love kids. All the kids, and now I have a nephew and when we…"

I can hear him talking, but a heat wave rushes through me, and every part of me begins to sweat as my heart races.

Reminding me of my past. Reminding me that there are things he doesn't know. A future he won't have. Of… of…

"I have to pee," I cut him off and run into the bathroom.

CHAPTER TWENTY-TWO
BECK - VEGAS

I'm a married man.

Beck and Calla Robertson.

Honestly, this is probably the best decision I ever made. Maybe all my choices from here on out need to be quick. No overthinking. If I want it, I take it.

I lean my head back against the wall and grin like a fool. All these people inserting their tickets into machines, hoping to win more money than they lose, have no idea how my life just changed for the better.

The guys are going to flip when I tell them.

I pull my phone from my pocket and open the group text.

No, that's lame. I'm not telling them in a text.

Especially not Simon. Hell, he's going to freak out when we tell him. I married his little sister, for crying out loud. He won't be particularly impressed with me.

A woman passes me, yelling at someone on the phone as she walks into the bathroom where Calla is currently.

When she excused herself, I snuck off to one of the

souvenir shops to buy us these glow-in-the-dark rings. Of course I'll get her a new one, a real one, when we get home. Right now, though, I just want to get her back to the room to celebrate.

I've never been so nervous and excited to be with someone in my entire life.

The loud-mouthed woman exits the bathroom, and I push off the wall.

Fuck, I hope Calla's okay in there. Hell, what if she got sick? We aren't drunk, but we've been steadily drinking for the last five hours.

I move to the doorway and call inside, "Calla, are you okay?"

A woman walks out, startling me to back up.

"There isn't anyone in there, buddy."

As soon as she's gone, I step inside to sneak in to see if she is telling me the truth. Then my phone buzzes with a text.

Calla: I'm sorry.

CHAPTER TWENTY-THREE
CALLA

I'm taking the very, *very* bad advice my three friends have given me and putting it to the test. But first, I stop to look into the mirror.

A lot of factors play into why I chose this route, but the biggest one is that after I confessed yesterday to not having a job, he has the upper hand now. I can't have that. Nope. Not even a little. If I can just show him that being half naked and keeping my hands to myself around him can happen, maybe it'll click that I'm not into him the way he is me.

The trick, though, is not giving in if he tries anything.

I can do this.

I tuck a loose strand of hair behind my ear. My outfit is simple. A plain white V-neck T-shirt that hangs off one shoulder. It's a little oversized, so it covers most of my butt. *Most of* being the key phrase here. I've got a pair of slate-blue bikini panties on, and I know that you can see them through the shirt. That's the point. He wants to use his body to unease me—well, joke's on him. Two can play this game, but only one will win, and I intend for that to be me.

Except… I cover my face and sit back on my bed. This is wild. What am I doing? This isn't me. I can't do this. I need to just suck it up and go get divorce papers. I'm a grown woman. So what if I don't have it all figured out?

Playing this game of who can drive the other crazier isn't going to get me anywhere. I'll put on some pants and go out there and tell him that I'll see an attorney in the morning, and this will all be over. I'll apologize for the tricks I've been playing and return everything I bought with his money. I'll find a job as soon as I can, a place of my own, and be out of his hair.

I'm almost thirty. I should have done this a long time ago.

It may have taken me this long, but hey, at least I figured it—

A loud crash upstairs startles me, and I stand quickly.

"Fuck!" Beck yells. "Fucking hell!"

Without thinking twice, I rush out of my room and up to the kitchen to find Beck standing over the sink with a towel over his hand. The towel is supposed to be white, but it's crimson now, the obvious blood from his hand changing the color.

"Are you okay?" I grab the towel to help add pressure.

"I cut my hand with the—"

He stops talking, so I look at his face to make sure he isn't about to turn into a ghost and pass out. There is no way I'd catch him before he hits the floor, but he's just fine. Well, if you forget about the clenched jaw and the heated gaze as his eyes roam over my entire body.

Oh. Right. The T-shirt and panties look.

Damn. I was so close to making the grown-up choice.

"I, um." I look at his hand. If I keep looking at the way he's looking at me, like I'm completely naked and he could eat me for a snack, I'm not sure I can hold it together. I'd let him.

"Do you have a first aid kit anywhere?" I manage to ask.

Is it normal for the heart to beat as hard as mine is right now? I swear, it feels like my chest is visibly moving with each pound.

Beck clears his throat as if he had to break some kind of trance before he says, "Top shelf in my bathroom."

"Okay, I'll be right back."

I walk as quickly as I can to the bathroom and find the kit, grab a thicker hand towel just in case, and return to the kitchen.

Beck hasn't moved.

"Maybe you should sit down," I say. I place a hand on his back to move him toward the table.

Really, Calla, he cut his hand. He doesn't need you touching him and helping him to a table.

"Do you know what you're doing?" he asks as I open the kit.

"Nope. But clearly neither did you," I snap back quickly.

I dampen the towel, cleaning up the cut before grabbing some gauze and a large Band-Aid.

"I don't think it needs stitches."

"Neither do I," he agrees and then laughs. "Of all the things I thought would be the first thing we agree on, it wasn't a steak knife cut on my hand."

I smile. "Well, yes, there are many other things you could

have done to gain my attention to have a simple conversion, but this worked well for you.”

“Oh, you think I did this on purpose?”

“I mean, you’ve cut food before, and it wasn’t a problem. I think you wanted to end the silent treatment, and this was a sure way to do it.”

“Okay, okay, and what was your way?” He tugs at the hem of my shirt, his fingers brushing daringly close to my panties, causing my fingers to tremble as I finish up his hand. “Tease me till I changed my mind?”

I bite my lip. “Maybe.”

“Mm, and what was your plan if the teasing went too far?”

The same hand that had tugged my shirt moments ago grazes the back of my thigh, moving down, up, barely touching my butt cheeks before he does it again.

I close my eyes and take a breath. I can’t think clearly for a response right now. His touch easily awakens something inside me, and I find myself desperate for him to keep going.

“How far?” I manage to say. “I… didn’t… think…”

“Of course you didn’t.” He leans forward. “What are you thinking now?”

What the hell? How can he think and say full sentences all while I’m trying not to combust right here, showing him how long it’s been since a man made me feel as crazy as he is right now. Making me think that for one night I could forget the past, all the games, all the problems between us and just let myself be here in the moment. Taking whatever he wants to give me.

“I’m not thinking,” I finally answer.

“Good.”

With the bandaged hand, he touches my hip ever so

gently, until I'm standing directly in front of him. Then, just as swiftly, he nudges my legs apart and pulls me into his lap.

I gasp, in a good way, and I definitely do not resist.

"Still not thinking?"

"Mm-hmm."

"Open your eyes, Calla," he says, his free hand moving to cup my cheek.

I do as he says, our eyes locking immediately.

His thumb brushes over my bottom lip. "God, your lips are perfect, and this pink gloss you have on them—I can't peel my eyes away."

"Do you like it?"

"Like it, Calla? I love it. Hell, my mind is racing with all the things I want those lips to do to me. With all the parts of my body I want to see them touch."

I swallow, taking a breath at his words. I want that too.

I relax in his lap and move my hips, a soft grind that does just enough to make both of us moan.

"I take that as a sign you want those lips to touch me, too?"

"Shut up, Beck," I say, finally finding my words. "Do you want to torture me by telling me more about the things you want to do to me, or do you want to actually do them?"

The small twitch of his lips tells me he wants to smile, but his expression quickly turns heated. His hands grab my hips, and he jerks me forward and back.

"Oh god," I breathe out. I can feel how hard he is beneath me. If you had asked me two months ago if I thought I'd be here, in Beck Robertson's kitchen, grinding on him at the table, I would have laughed in your face. Yet here I am, and I honestly don't want to be anywhere else.

Our situation is already complicated, and this, whatever is happening, will only make it worse.

I stall my hips to bring this to his attention, but he kisses me before I can say a single word. It's gentle at first, but once his tongue slips through my lips and I feel his groan vibrate against me—well, we earned a little fun, didn't we?

I kiss him back, my fingers weaving through his thick dark hair, holding on as every action between us becomes rushed. In a swift motion, Beck is standing and setting me on the table. His lips never leave mine as he leans me back. Once my head is on the table, his lips move from mine to my neck. He yanks my shirt until my white lace bra is visible, and then he kisses lower—and lower.

Oh, this is happening. It feels so good.

Once he reaches my breast, he pulls my bra back, sucking on my nipple like his life depends on it.

"Sit up," he says. I quickly do as he says because I'll do whatever he wants if it means I can keep feeling the way I am right now. Reckless and sedated and at peace all at the same time. It sounds crazy. But that's how it is with Beck. I can feel out of control every moment of every day, and yet I'm right where I need to be.

He lifts my shirt over my head, doing the same to himself before he unclasps my bra, dropping it to the floor.

"If I'd have known that being shirtless would gain me that smile, I would have started doing it a lot more."

"Stop." I roll my eyes, but yeah, I like looking at his chest.

"Stop what?" he asks, yanking me to the edge of the table and tugging my panties off. "Undressing you?" Then he takes my breast in his mouth again, and my head drops back.

"Sucking on you?" I hear his belt buckle, followed by the shuffle of clothes hitting the floor. "Or devouring you?"

I don't get a chance to interpret that last one before he drops to his knees and puts his mouth on me. I buckle over him, all while trying not to cry out like some untouched beginner.

His tongue begins to flick faster, and that sensation of my soon-to-be-released orgasm zings through me.

"Beck." His name is a whisper off my lips, and the mere sound of my voice causes him to increase his pace. Oh god. I never… I never…

An explosion rips through me, and I cry out. Beck stands quickly, two fingers replacing his lips.

"Fuck!" My scream is silenced by his mouth. I grip his shoulders to hold on as he curls his fingers inside me, prolonging my orgasm and causing my entire body to shake.

Hell. I've never come so hard in my entire life.

Everything begins to slow down, and as soon as I've caught my breath a little, I reach for him.

He grunts as soon as my hand covers his hard length.

"Calla, you don't have to do that, or anything. I just—"

"I want you, Beck. I want this. Do you?"

I never take my eyes off him. We've spent too much time not telling the other one exactly what we want. If ever there was a place to change that, it's right now.

"You're sure?" he asks.

I groan and nudge him closer with my heel to his butt. The tip of his cock touches my entrance, and we both suck in a breath.

"There's no going back after this," he says. "You're mine."

"I know," I say and kiss him.

He slowly starts to push inside me when the doorbell rings.

"Shit," he hisses and pulls out, jerking his pants up. "Shit. Shit. Shit."

"What? Just don't answer it."

"It's Wednesday," he says, as if I should know exactly what that means. He starts rushing around the table and tosses my clothes at me. "Get dressed."

"I'm sorry," I snap and hop off the table. "I didn't realize there was something else you'd rather be doing."

I pull my shirt over my head and step into my panties.

"You're reading this wrong," he says and then pulls me by the hip toward him and kisses me.

I shove him back. "You just stopped mid-sex with me because your doorbell rang. I didn't read anything wrong."

"Calla," he says with a warning. "Trust me when I say I'd love nothing more than to be deep inside you right now, but if—"

The doorbell rings again, and then the door handle jiggles.

"Beck, open the door. Why is it locked anyway? You never lock it."

My eyes widen at the sound of my brother's voice.

"It's Wednesday," I repeat as their weekly group writing finally clicks into place.

Beck is just getting himself put back together as I escape down the stairs.

It feels like I don't take my next breath until I'm in my room with the door closed.

My brother almost caught his best friend going down on me, and more, at the kitchen table.

Oh. My. God.

Oh. My. God.

Oh. My. God.

I repeat this about a dozen times before I go upstairs for a glass of water. I repeat it once more, mouthing it to Beck as he flashes me a cheeky grin. Then I see my brother sitting at the end of the table. At *that* end.

If I thought my life was complicated before when it came to Beck Robertson, I'm in for one hell of a ride now.

CHAPTER TWENTY-FOUR
BECK

It's occurred to me that I've been so focused on building a career all these years that I've never actually been in a long-term relationship, and living with Calla the past few weeks and being married these past few months has well turned into my longest relationship.

I'm not sure what I'm doing, but from my experience and from the feedback I've received from the books I've written, I have a sneaking good feeling that buying gifts randomly for women is always a wise move.

It's silly, but when I was buying new supplies for my office, I saw this planner that made me think of Calla.

Okay, so I had to resort to what my heroes would do, due to the simple fact that the guys were over till almost two in the morning. I can only think of a handful of times the weekly group night went that late. It usually stems from one of us nearing a deadline and needing as much help as we can get during a plot hole. Last night was no different.

Graham's book is due by Friday, and apparently, his new neighbors are a huge pain in his ass, so he asked if he could stay late to write where he knew he'd get some quiet time. So he was there for a reason, and the fact that I almost just had sex with Calla wasn't it.

I could have easily said I was going to my office and then gone to her room, but then what? I just show up in her room ready for her to pick up where we left off because I was available now? That's not fair to her.

Hence, buying an apology gift.

She was gone before I woke up today. Where? No clue.

I could simply text how sorry I am for ignoring her after what went down with us, but something shifted between us yesterday, and Calla deserves more than an "I'm sorry I couldn't have sex with you because my friends came over" text.

I knew it was her brother when the doorbell rang yesterday. Simon is always the first to arrive. We usually hang out for a bit before we write. It never occurred to me until the second ring that, if this works out between me and Calla, what will Simon think?

I panicked a little.

Just because we're best friends doesn't mean he wants me to be that guy for his sister. I mean, we are guys; we still need to talk about relationship stuff, you know. How would I do that with Simon?

It would be weird for him, and how would that affect our friendship?

Yesterday was both one of the best days of my life and also filled my mind with more questions than I have answers for.

I leave the small local shop where I got Calla's planner and then walk a few stores down to Love's a Brewing for some coffee and to see if my sister is around. She pops in late afternoons sometimes once she finishes her day at Wind Valley Elementary. She and her fiancé, Will, own the coffee shop. It's connected to our local bookstore, where they offer a deal for coffee and books to any student who shows them ID. It's pretty genius, and it's also nice to have my sister living in the same town as me again. When she graduated from high school and ran off to college, I had this sickening feeling she wouldn't be back. But she is, and her best friend, thank god for him, finally made sure she stayed this time.

I push the door open, the smell of fresh ground coffee beans filling the air. My soon-to-be brother-in-law once told me this specific smell reminded him of success. Seeing as how I associate the smell with wanting to pull out my laptop and write a couple new scenes, he's not wrong.

"Beck!" my sister squeals and comes around the counter to hug me. "How are you?"

"I'm good, and yourself?"

Hands on hips, she nods and smiles. "Can't complain. Except maybe that you don't come in nearly enough to see me."

"Phones work both ways," I tease her, but she's right. Even though we live in the same town, we don't make nearly enough time for each other as we should.

"Well, if anyone knows what it's like to work hard to make your dream succeed, it's you."

I follow her toward the register.

"Will has really come a long way with this place—it's amazing."

"You and your friends should do some of your writing nights here," she suggests.

"We tried that once before this place opened, and we spent more time being approached by fans or people we knew. We didn't get much done."

"Oh, your *fans*." She rolls her eyes. "Wind Valley isn't big enough to be bombarded by fans, Beck."

"That doesn't mean we don't have them."

"Probably more than in Melody. That's no joke. Especially when it comes to the local bookstore."

She slides a black coffee toward me with a laugh, and I hand her cash. She waves me off, so I drop it in the tip jar.

The local bookstore in Melody she's referring to is to the one that Calla and Simon's parents own. Calla once mentioned that she didn't like my books, and my sister has never let it go. She loves to remind me every chance she gets. Little does she know.

A few more people trickle in, so I say a quick goodbye. It's when I step outside that a thought occurs to me. My sister might be a good person for me to confide in about my current situation.

Then again, it's probably best not to bring family into this. Especially not mine. If any of them find out I'm married, they will freak out. Not in the "you got married without us" way. More of the "yay, we can't believe it! Let's celebrate" way. Which is great, yeah, if both parties actually want to be married.

Which brings me to another question that has appeared since yesterday's fondle session with Calla. Where does this leave us when it comes to our marriage? Now, I'm not an idiot. Just because I can make her come with my mouth doesn't mean she automatically wants to stay married. It might, however, be a start to convincing her to stay.

My heart clenches with a new feeling. Fear.

It hits me so hard that I stop in the middle of the sidewalk, causing someone to bump into me. They mumble something but keep moving.

Before this moment, I wanted Calla to stay so we could see if there was something between us. Now I want her to stay because there is. No more guessing.

Fuck.

I let out a breath and walk the rest of the way to my car.

If she leaves, who will arrange the pillows on the couch to fit just right against my lower back? Who will put the remote back where it belongs so I can find it every time I need it? Who will light the vanilla candle in the kitchen so that it smells like someone has been baking? Who will come barging into my office when I'm bouncing the ball off the wall just to yell at me and get me all worked up?

It's stupid things, probably, but they're the little things about her I want to keep. The little things that become the big things because they are what make Calla her.

"Hey, Beck."

I glance up to see Tobias and Graham standing in front of me. Tobias tilts his head, and a smile slowly appears on lips.

"What are you doing?"

His curious tone makes me look around, and it's only then I notice I'm just standing next to my car.

"Nothing."

"I called your name three times. You've been standing here the entire time."

Well, hell.

I open my mouth to make up an excuse, but fuck, I need someone to know what's happening in my life. I need someone to talk to, and Graham is on the phone.

"I married Calla in Vegas over the summer and now she lives with me, and at first, I was just trying to get her stay with me because I didn't want divorce clinging to my reputation as a romance writer, but also because I didn't want to be the first in my family to get divorced. Then I touched her last night, and she touched me, and I think I'm gone for her." I run a hand through my hair. "I fell for my wife."

There's a pause of about ten seconds before Tobias lets out a bark of laughter.

"It's not funny."

"Well, it's not *not* funny."

I slouch against my driver's door and hold up the bag.

"I got her a gift today."

"Cool, what is it?"

"A planner," I say with confidence.

"A planner?"

I nod.

"Like, a month-to-month planner?"

I shove his shoulder, and he laughs.

"She likes this kind of stuff. Being organized and whatnot."

I shake my head and unlock my car.

"Hey." Tobias reaches out to stop me. He's smiling, but I can see in his eyes that he's about to say something serious. "I secretly always hoped she'd come around for you."

"What?"

He nods. "For years. The tension between you two has

always been electric, and it never went unnoticed by the group. Simon, maybe, but that's because she's his sister, and I think guys tend to not get that type of energy off their sisters."

At that, I laugh.

"But to the rest of us, this is great. Really. Congratulations, and let me know if I can help at all or if you just want to talk."

"Thanks, man. I'll take you up on it."

"See you later."

"See you—oh hey," I call out as Graham ends his calls and is following Tobias. "Did you ever finish unpacking your apartment?"

He shakes his head. "Six months later and no. Between deadlines and book signings, the idea of figuring out where everything goes exhausts me."

"What do you think of paying Calla to do it?"

"To unpack my shit?"

I roll my eyes. "To unpack and decorate your place. Organize it. Set it up. She loves to do that kind of stuff and I think she could make a career out of it."

A huge smile takes over his face.

"Ah, what now?"

"Nothing." He shakes his head. "I'd love to hire her. Have her get me a quote."

My heart hammers in my chest. If she doesn't like the planner, this is a great backup.

"Thanks, man."

"No problem. See you next Wednesday."

I get in my car and rush home.

Calla's car is here when I pull up. Of course it is. Now that

I know she doesn't have a job, she doesn't have to pretend all day. Shit. I should have noticed sooner. I hate that she felt she had to hide that from me—or anyone.

I park next to her, failing miserably not to grin like a fool at the idea of always coming home to park next to her.

As soon as I walk in the front door, the scent of vanilla fills the air, and yeah, there is no hiding this smile.

"You're home," Calla says before I even have the door closed. She stands from the couch and turns off the TV. "I think we should talk about last night."

She looks nervous, and even though I heard her, I'm too excited to wait to share my own news. On impulse, I kiss her mouth.

She doesn't stop me, but her widening eyes tell me she wasn't expecting it.

Her fingers touch her lips after I pull back.

"I have a surprise for you," I tell her and hand her the bag with her planner. "I also bought you this."

She slowly reaches for the bag and pulls out the planner. Then, she smiles. She sits back down and flips through it.

I swallow the lump in my throat because she never stops grinning.

"Why do I love this?" She looks up and laughs. "It's a planner, and yet, I don't know, it feels like this is exactly what I needed."

"There's more," I say and sit next to her.

"More? Beck, you didn't need to even buy me this. Actually, this is a great way to segue this conversation into what happened yesterday."

"Okay, and I promise we can talk about it, but let me share this with you first."

Her eyes search mine, and instead of arguing, she nods. "Okay, go."

"Even though you reorganized my entire house in an attempt to get under my skin," she wrinkles her nose with a small smile, "my house looks amazing, and everything is organized beautifully. I think you should turn that into a real job, start your own business. I even found you your first client. It's Graham. He still isn't unpacked, and he hates the idea of putting everything away. Shoot, last time I was at his house, he only had one set of utensils out of the box. He wants you to get him a quote."

The smile that was just brightening her face falls, and she stares at me.

Shit. That was too much. I came off too strong. Hell, now that I think about it, I basically made it seem like she was going to do this when it's really only an idea in my head.

After what feels like an eternity passes and she hasn't said a word, I clear my throat. "Shit. I'm sorry. I… you wanted to talk about last night."

Her mouth opens, but she closes it without a word.

My instinct tells me to just get up and go—go anywhere else. But the other half of me says that's a dick move to leave her here before she's had a chance to say anything.

Luckily for me, she doesn't make me wait much longer.

"You… you bought me a planner and got me a job organizing someone's apartment." It's not a question. It's a statement. She looks at the clock on the wall and back to me. "It's not even noon."

I rub the back of my neck and nod. "Yeah, I…"

"Thank you!" she exclaims and leaps toward me, wrapping her arms around me. She squeezes me tight for a brief moment before releasing me and pressing her lips to mine. "Thank you."

We kiss one more time before she gets up.

"Wait," I call out. "Where are you going?"

"To start a business," she says with a wink and disappears down the steps.

CHAPTER TWENTY-FIVE
CALLA

Very few things shock me anymore. But let me tell you, Beck Robertson just blew my mind.

I'd stayed up way too late last night thinking. By the time I fell asleep, I'd decided that my focus needed to be on a job and a place to live, not obsessing over whether Beck somehow magically felt the same way I did after one moment together.

As soon as I was awake and showered this morning, I'd gone upstairs to find him. To talk about yesterday and to tell him that it's probably best we just forget about it and go on with our lives. As friends. Yep, I had the whole "let's just be friends" speech ready to go. Then I panicked and left. I drove around for an hour trying to put my thoughts together.

But then, oh my gosh, he came home today, and… just wow.

He bought me a planner and he got me a job. Beck paid enough attention to me since I've moved in to see how much I enjoy organizing and moving things around to find their perfect spot. He legit had the same exact thought I did about making this into a business. Here I thought he was… it doesn't matter. I was wrong.

I settle onto my bed, legs crossed with my laptop in front of me and planner in my lap. Three pens to my left in purple, black, and blue. I have the website up for starting a business in Wyoming. First, I just need—

"Calla," Beck's voice comes through my door after a single knock.

I jump up and open it, and his eyes roam slowly to take me in. I've got on a plain black shirt and shorts, so my legs and arms are all the skin he gets. After yesterday, I know how quickly things can escalate.

"I just wanted to say that I'm going to be writing in my office for a bit, and if you want a place to sit that isn't your bed, you're welcome to use the other half of my desk."

Oh lordy. Why is he so cute?

"You want me to come work with you in your office?"

He nods.

Not sitting on my bed will probably make me more productive, but that's his office. His writing cave. It feels intimate to intrude for actual work. Like I might steal the energy or something.

"You know, that's actually a good idea, but I don't want to invade your space. I can just use the table upstairs."

He bites his bottom lip and smiles.

A flash of him standing over me at the table comes to mind, and suddenly, I think I know what he's thinking.

"Okay, well, my office is open if you change your mind."

"Thanks," I say all too quickly.

He turns to leave, and it doesn't take me long to realize

that sitting at that table trying to work will be pointless because I'll only be able to think of last night.

A few minutes later, I'm walking into his office and taking the chair across from him.

"I'll never look at that table the same way again."

His head drops back with a bark of laughter. "You and me both."

Our gazes collide. I shake my head and point my finger at him. "No."

"I didn't say a word," he says, holding his hands up in surrender.

"You didn't have to. I know that look. It says, 'Hey, how about we remember this desk the way we remember the kitchen table?'"

"Well, that wasn't exactly what I was thinking, but now it is." He laughs again.

"Uh-huh, sure, so what were you thinking?"

He hesitates. "I was thinking that I like this. Having you in here while I work. Your presence calms me."

"Oh."

"Yeah, I'm a little shocked too. Actually, this might be a good time to tell you about—"

I cut him off with a shake of my head and then look at my screen. "Get to work," I say and start filling in what I can for this application.

Two hours pass quickly, and suddenly, Beck is standing.

"Do you want anything to drink?" he asks.

"Oh, sure." I blink and then lean back. "I'll come with you. I need a break."

"How is it going?"

"It's a lot of research and a lot of steps to start a business."

My brain is fried trying to keep it all straight.

"True, but you'll get it."

We reach the kitchen, and he moves for the fridge, and I head for the snack drawer. We both grab a couple things and head back down the stairs. Neither of us says a word about who wants what. But oddly enough, we both seem satisfied with what the other chose.

Beck sits back in his chair, but I opt for the corner of his desk. I need a few more minutes away from the bright light that's slowly melting my eyeballs.

"I don't know how you can look at a screen this much in a day."

"You get used to it."

"Yeah, probably. I bet—what's that? Why are you looking at me like that? What now?"

He's so easy to read. I hate that I love it.

He chuckles and grabs his neck. "Honestly?"

"Yes, please."

"I'm thinking I don't want to be on my computer right now. I don't want to think about this book." The fire in his gaze keeps me from asking what he'd rather be doing. I know.

Me. That's what.

I clear my throat and slip off the edge of his desk. I could leave him and work alone—it's definitely a smart choice—but a new feeling washes over me.

I don't want to leave. I like being around Beck. I like the way I feel around him. I like that he believes in me. I like that we can just be together, and it feels right.

Instead of playing games or doing my usual MO, I take the route I should have taken weeks ago. I spin around and use my words.

"Won't this complicate things?" I ask.

"What do you mean?"

"I mean, I want to be doing what you're thinking we should be doing, but we're married, Beck."

He chuckles, and I glare at him.

"If that weren't a factor, would you still want me?" he asks.

"Yes."

"Then let's just put the fact we're married to the side for now. We're doing this because we want to, not because of a piece of paper."

"I know, but what happens if—"

"Don't think about it, Calla. I have no idea what tomorrow holds, but today there is us, and that's where I want to be."

Us.

I think I like the sound of that.

Slowly, I walk toward him. He turns in his chair, reaching for me.

As soon as I straddle his lap, he captures my lips with his own and kisses me like a man starved. He holds onto me as if I'm his lifeboat. It sounds so silly, but kissing Beck is where I'm meant to be, and I can't believe I fought it for so long.

Without breaking the kiss, Beck stands, holding me at my rear, and walks us to my room. He sits on the bed and lies back with me on top.

"For the record," he says, "after this, you're not sleeping anywhere but in my bed. Got it?"

"Yes." I lift my shirt over my head. He sits up to do the same. Once we're both topless, he flips us over and starts unbuttoning my jeans.

"I've been thinking of this moment for too damn long, Calla."

"Since Vegas?"

"Before. I just never thought it was a reality till Vegas."

"I thought you always hated me."

"Never." He kisses down my neck and pulls my nipple into his mouth.

Oh god.

"I just liked seeing you worked up. So I fed off your energy."

"That's kind of twisted," I tell him. "And I think I like it."

The vibration of his laugh touches my chest, causing me to buck my hips. He jerks my pants and underwear the rest of the way off. Then he pulls a condom out of his wallet and tosses his pants to the floor.

"Oh," I say and nod to the small packet. "We don't need that. We're good."

The smile on his lips makes my heart race.

"Are you sure?"

"Positive."

He kisses me again as he slowly pushes inside me.

"Oh god," I gasp out. "Wow."

He pulls back out on a groan and slams back into me.

Holy shit. He's huge. He's just like I imagined after feeling him the other day. This is incredible.

He pulls out, and I itch to reach for him, but he buries his face between my legs before I can protest his absence. He licks me once.

"Beck. Oh my god."

His tongue works quickly, and my body responds even faster.

Like before, he stops. I pop my eyes open to ask why he still loves to torture me, but he slides back inside me in one hard thrust.

Yes!

Over and over he repeats this process. Licking me and then fucking me.

Over and over and over. Each position brings me right to the edge before he switches.

"Baby, you feel so good."

"I feel good." I pant. "God, you're driving me absolutely mad."

"I'm about to come. Can you come with me?"

"Yes," I breathe.

He picks up the pace, and I can feel it, the current coursing through my veins and turning my vision white.

"Calla!" Beck calls out just as my orgasm kidnaps my entire body. I have no control over what it does for the next thirty seconds.

"Holy shit," I say when my vision returns.

"Holy shit," Beck says, lying next to me. We both laugh as he pulls me in close.

"Give me five minutes, and we are doing that again."

A giddy sensation swallows my heart.

I will take as much as he wants to give.

CHAPTER TWENTY-SIX

BECK

Keeping my hands to myself is nearly impossible these days. In all the moments when I thought about how staying married was important to me, I never realized how much more important it would be to me to be happily married.

And right now, the idea that I'm married to the woman standing in my kitchen spraying Cool Whip into her mouth does things to me that I never imagined. I want to lick the cream right out of her mouth. I want to take the can and spray it on parts of her body that don't require food. I want her to sleep in my bed and wake up next to me and I want... her. I want her right here with me. Always.

She starts to put the can back in the door of the fridge but then thinks better of it and gives herself one more shot.

I can't help but chuckle behind her.

With whip cream on the corners of her lips, she spins around and starts to laugh.

"Attractive, right?" she says with a mouthful.

"More than you think."

I approach her, her gaze studying my every move.

"I have to leave in about twenty minutes," she says and sticks her hand out. "Do not start something you cannot finish before that time is up."

"Twenty minutes is plenty of time."

"Beck," she coos in a flirtatious tone.

"Calla." I grab the can from her, pressing my lips to hers. I snake a hand around her waist and pull her close, spinning as I do this. Then I grab her by the ass and plop her on the counter.

"This kitchen has seen more action than any kitchen I've ever known," she says between kisses. "Should we move to a more private place?"

"What's more private than our own house?"

She answers me with another kiss.

I grab the can of Cool Whip and spray her neck before she can even notice what I'm doing.

"Beck, that… ah" is all she says before my tongue is licking every last bit. "Just the neck?"

I growl and tug at her shirt.

"To start."

Together we pull her shirt off only to be stopped by her phone ringing.

"I need to get that."

"Make it quick."

She blushes but nods.

"Hey, I'm about to leave my house," she answers. I'd complain because it's a clear statement that whatever we were about to start has to wait till later, but *my house* hits me right in the chest.

Maybe her choice of words is a hint to where this new

relationship is going.

"Okay, see you soon."

She hangs up and then sticks her bottom lip out. "I have to go."

"I know. Does it make me a bad person that I liked this past week when you didn't have a job and our main focus was me and the bed we share?"

She laughs. "It was a great week, but this is big for me."

Graham hired Calla, and she's been working nonstop. She'll finish at his place today, and she told me last night that she can't wait to get pictures for her portfolio.

"I know. I'm proud of you."

She freezes as I kiss her forehead. "You good?" I ask.

She nods. "Yes." Then she kisses me so hard that I'm reaching for her clothes, wishing she would come back as she walks out the door.

I let out a sigh, crossing my arms and leaning against the counter as I stare at the front door.

It feels freeing to be this happy.

Alright, we'll pick this back up when she comes home.

I grab my computer and head to my office.

Today is the day I tell Doug that we should accept HBO's offer.

Fuck. I'm nervous, but it's clear that I'm not going to have a new book in time for a movie deal with HBO. Come on, that's something to check off my bucket list. I can't turn it down.

Obviously, I need to tell Calla about the book. I wrote a novel based on our story and it turned out so well that two of the biggest movie streamers out there want to buy it and play it for the whole world to see. It sounds harmless. But if I've learned anything about Calla since we moved in, she doesn't trust easily. I just got her—I can't mess it up. The way I see it, it'll take weeks, months even, before anything is announced or revealed. I have time to tell her.

Right now, while we're in the honeymoon stage if you will, isn't the time to tell her.

I get situated at my desk, shoot Doug an email to tell him to get the contracts going, and then lean back. Everything will work out. Being with Calla is right, and signing this movie deal is right.

I cross my arms and smile at my unfinished office.

Hiring Calla to finish putting this room together was also the right choice.

I jump up. I should keep working, but there's one more thing Calla doesn't know about.

The surprise birthday party I'm having tonight here at the house. Her birthday isn't till tomorrow, so hopefully, she has no idea.

I grab my keys, the list of errands I need to run, and the application I picked up yesterday for Calla. Well, for her gift. Which will be late and might be a little presumptuous of me, but we will find out in a few weeks.

For now, I just want tonight to be perfect for my girl.

* * *

"I've got to hand it to you, man, this is pretty cool."

Simon steps out onto my back patio and clasps a hand on my shoulder. It's chilly out here, but this is where the grill is, so I'm here till the food is done.

"Yeah, there are still some days where I can't believe I own this place."

He grunts. "I'm talking about this party you put together for my sister. One might think the two of you have become friends since she moved in."

"Yeah, I guess."

"You guess?" He laughs. "Leave it to you and my sister to become friends but never actually admit it out loud."

I see where my reaction could lead him to think this, but I'm working on the courage to ask him what I really want.

"Can I ask you something about your sister and you promise you won't get mad?"

"Umm, with that lead-in, I can't promise you a damn thing."

I roll my eyes and crack the grill to see if the burgers are almost done.

"Would you be upset if I asked your sister out on a date?"

He twirls the beer bottle in his hand. "Like a real date? Like a kiss her at the end of the night date?"

I smile. "Yes."

He doesn't say anything right away, and his blank expression gives me nothing.

"Does she know you like her?"

I volley my head side to side. "I think she does, yeah."

"And she's cool with it? Being in a relationship?"

"Does she have something against them?"

"I didn't say that. I was just asking."

"Look, we've made comments here and there, but I think the both of us would be more comfortable if we knew you were cool with it."

"Oh yeah. Of course I am. You two are such complete opposites that it's almost perfect. Just take it slow, alright?"

I hold back my laughter as I move the burgers to a plate to take inside. Slow isn't exactly the word I'd use to describe Calla and me.

We step into the house, and chatter fills the air. I immediately spot Calla with Greer, and my body perks to attention.

A thought that never occurred to me till this moment: how am I going to not touch Calla while we're surrounded by our friends? Calla's parents weren't able to make it, but judging by the smile on her face, I did a pretty good job. But still, no peppered kisses and subtle brushes of my hand against her butt when I walk behind her?

I didn't think this through.

"A surprise party, huh?" Graham elbows me in the kitchen. "Things must be going okay in the romance department."

"Shhh." I glance around for wherever Simon ventured off to. "She hasn't said anything to her brother yet."

Do I wish she would? Yes. Am I going to pressure her to tell him? No.

"But yes, things with Calla are going well. Great actually."

"Ah, shit."

"What?"

"Another one of you is tied down. I honestly thought you'd be the first, but all good things take time, right?"

I chuckle. Looks like it.

"Are you thinking about settling down?" I ask. Graham doesn't talk about his personal life too much, so even if he were casually dating, I don't think I would know about it.

He's not the type of guy to just come right out and say he's in a relationship.

He shrugs.

"I want to be a little more advanced in my career before I settle down."

"Smart."

I'm glad one of us knows what's up and how to keep a lockdown on their writing life.

Calla walks by me, her hand grazing my back gently. I watch her every step only to catch her biting her bottom lip.

Fuck this.

"Calla, a word."

"Of course." She turns around and follows me out of the kitchen.

I peek over my shoulder to see that no one is paying attention to us.

"Come with me." I grab her hand and rush down the hall with her giggling quietly behind me.

"Beck, someone is going to see us and figure this out."

"I don't really care right now. I just want you."

The sparkle in her shines for a moment before she shuts the door behind me.

"Lay on your back."

Her tone is more demanding this time. But I do exactly as I'm told. She reaches down to the hem of her shirt, pulling it off as she climbs on the bed, stands on the mattress and puts a foot on my hand when I try to remove my own shirt.

"Don't you dare remove that shirt."

I glance up at her standing above me, and it all clicks.

"You are not doing this," I say with a giant smile.

"Oh, I'm doing it. And so are you."

She grabs her skirt at the sides and scrunches it up before standing over my face.

"Holy shit. You've already removed your panties. Fuck, baby, look at you."

Just when I think I'm in control of the situation, she grips the back of the headboard and lowers herself to my mouth.

"Oh shit," she moans at the first swipe of my tongue.

This, right here, is becoming a favorite of mine. Sex with Calla is the best thing ever, but when my face is between her legs, I can't help but feel crazed. Everything just goes white, and nothing matters but what I'm doing to her.

Her chest rises and falls rapidly as my mouth moves faster.

"Oh god, Beck. I'm so close."

"Good," I say, barely coming up for air to say it.

"I don't want to come like this. I want you inside me."

I don't have to be told twice. In one swift motion, I slide from under her and flip us over. I'm on top of her and tugging my jeans off before I can take my next breath.

"Whatever the birthday girl wants, she gets."

I push into her in a single thrust. She cries out so loudly that I slap a hand over her mouth. Her eyes are wide. I start to move my hand, thinking I might have been too rough, but she stops me.

My hips grind slowly into her as she lifts her own to deepen our connections.

"Fuck," I let out on a whisper.

Calla's hands reach down to cup my ass, jerking me faster.

I take the hint and do just what she wants.

I start to pound into her, her cries muffled by my hand.

She bites me as she draws closer.

I'd slow us down and let us enjoy every minute of this bliss, but our friends are waiting, and this is not the way I want them to find out about Calla and me.

She moves her hand from my butt to touch herself, and when I see her rubbing her clit, I explode, the sensation pulling her own orgasm from her at the same time.

I collapse and roll off her so that I don't crush her.

She curls to her side and kisses my chest.

"I'm loving this party, but I sort of wish we didn't have people here right now."

I chuckle.

"Me too, babe. Me too."

We both grab the clothes that we removed and quickly put ourselves back together.

"I'll go first," I told her. "It's my room. If someone sees me coming out, it won't raise questions."

"Smart."

She sits on my bed, grinning at me.

I take two long strides back to her and kiss her.

"I think I like you," I tell her, and she blushes.

"I think I like you too."

I head out back to the party, and ten minutes pass before Calla fakes coming down with something and pulls me back to the bedroom.

CHAPTER TWENTY-SEVEN
BECK

It's Wednesday, and the guys and I are sitting in a circle around the table at Tobias's house. Everyone is writing, including me.

Yep, that's right.

My spark is back, and it's hotter than ever.

I think we all know who to thank for that. Who knew that getting the girl and a movie deal would be all I needed to get back into the swing of things?

"Holy shit," Hero says, and everyone stops typing to look at him.

"What?" Zane asks. "You can't just interrupt like that and pause."

"Right." Hero shakes his head and looks at me. "I totally spaced this, but Doug mentioned you got a movie deal with HBO. That's amazing. Why didn't you say anything?"

The table erupts into congratulations and instant chatter about goals and books-to-movie adaptations. I thank them, praying none of them ask me—

"What's it about?" Simon asks.

That. I was hoping none of them asked me that.

"Oh, you know, just your standard enemies to lovers. Doug really upsold me."

I focus back on my computer, hoping the subject will change.

"Come on, man, tell us more," Zane says.

I shake my head and blow out a breath. How much do I share? Not all of them know what's happening in my life, and this sure as shit isn't the time to tell Simon. One, one-on-one is better and two, Calla should have a say on when that happens, so yeah, it's not happening now. The less I share, the better.

"Just a couple enemies who get drunk and then get married to each other. Should be a good romcom, and HBO will do it right. I'm thrilled."

"Classic," Simon says with a laugh. "HBO is definitely the right choice if you want to keep the type of steam you write in the storyline. And two people who hate each other and are forced to be together until they admit their feelings. That's hot."

I rub my burning neck, then look up. Tobias is shaking his head, and Graham looks like a kid at Christmas.

"Yeah, it's good." I look at my watch. "Shoot, you know what, I need to run. I have some, um, papers to look over for Doug for this movie, and I should probably do it while the topic is fresh in my mind."

The boys give me another round of congratulations, and Tobias walks me out.

"Is this for real?" he asks once we're outside. It's crisp out. And I bounce back and forth on my feet.

October in Wyoming is hit or miss. You could have camp-fire fall weather before bed and winter when you wake up. Given the temperature right now, I'm expecting snow in the morning.

I blow out a breath.

"It was an accident."

"Does Calla know?"

"Not yet."

"*Yet* being the key word here, right?"

"I'll tell her tonight."

Now that everyone knows about the movie deal, there's no way I couldn't tell her.

Hell, I should have told her the day I made the decision.

"Good." He smirks. "I've never seen you this… relaxed."

"Relaxed?"

"Yeah. Like, you don't seem in a hurry for much the last week or so. You're just enjoying each day as it comes. Calla is good for you." He winks. "You two need to come clean soon."

I grin. "Sneaking around is fun though."

He shoves my shoulder.

"Tell her."

"I am."

"Talk to you later, then."

He waves and heads inside. I climb into my SUV and head home.

"Beck!" Calla shouts from upstairs. "Beck, guess what?" Her voice grows louder, and I can hear the excitement in it. I meet her on the staircase as she comes racing down.

"What's up?"

"I got another job!"

"What?" I smile and pull her in for a kiss. "That's amazing."

"I know! Graham said his landlord needed to come fix the dishwasher, and when he saw the place, he complimented it, so Graham told him about me. Turns out, this guy not only has rental properties, but he's a Realtor, too, and he wants to meet me to see my portfolio. If he likes it, he wants me to stage a few houses for him. If he likes that, he wants a twelve-month contract."

"Holy shit, that's amazing."

"I know. I just—" Her eyes widen. "Three weeks ago, I had no idea what I was going to do with my days, and now, I just can't believe it." She pulls me in for a hug. "Thank you, Beck."

"I didn't do anything."

"You got me the work with Graham."

"You got you the work, Calla."

She grabs my shirt and pulls me in for a kiss. "I need to make a portfolio by Friday. Your house and Graham's are all I have to put in it."

Her shoulder drops at the thought, and that just won't do.

"What about Willa's studio? You've done things there."

"True."

"And," I pull out my phone, "I happen to have a sister and future brother-in-law who own a coffee shop. I could pull a few strings to see if they'd let you come in the next day or two. And my office needs a touch of your charm too. I've been meaning to ask you for a while now."

Her entire face lights up. "Why are you so good to me?"

"Because I like you."

She squeals.

"Hey, I need to talk to you about something," I say as she types away on her phone. "Do you remember that—"

"Hold that thought." She beams at me. "Willa said I could come right now for pictures."

"Oh yeah, of course, go."

"Do you want to come with me? We can talk in the car."

And chance ruining her mood on the good news? Not a chance.

"You'll be quicker without me. Go. Work and get your ass back here." I smack her butt and kiss her cheek.

She gives me a tight hug. "You're the best, Beck. I think I like you."

"I think I like you too," I tell her as she rushes out the door.

Which is exactly why tonight is not the night for me to tell her about the book.

CHAPTER TWENTY-EIGHT
CALLA

"You still owe me twenty bucks," Willa says, picking a fresh baked chocolate chip cookie off the cooling rack.

"Don't remind me," Greer says and does the same. They both sit at the kitchen island of Beck's kitchen while I prepare the next batch for the oven.

"You should owe me forty for the view we have now." Willa laughs. "She's cooking him dinner, and they've been fooling around for two maybe three weeks now."

"Good thing I only bet twenty. I didn't realize she was going to fall this hard."

"You two do know I can hear you, right?"

"Yep."

"Yes."

"Just checking." I put the tray in the oven, then check the second oven. Yes, there are two. When I said Beck had the house of my dreams, I wasn't lying.

"I think it's cute," Willa says.

"Of course you do. You're happy and in love. From my

view, my only two friends are dropping like flies into happy bliss."

Greer grabs her phone while Willa and I share a look.

"Has Matt still not returned your calls?" I ask. Greer has been on one bad date after the next. I can see how she would be frustrated right now. She mentioned taking a break from guys a while back, I think this breakup might be the one that puts that plan in motion.

"No, he hasn't. And you know what? It's not even that I liked him. It's the fact that he ghosted me. Why do people do that? Why can't they just grow a pair and say, hey, I don't think this is working for me?"

"Because boys suck," I say.

"Who sucks?" Simon says, walking into the kitchen.

"Simon," I point to the door, "there is a doorbell and this tall, square piece of wood that you knock on before walking into someone's house."

He smiles, winks at Willa and Greer, and takes a cookie. He gives Greer a quick glance. It was so fast, I almost missed it.

Huh? I know I asked Greer about dinner that night, but maybe I need to hear both sides.

"We have some things to finish up at the studio anyway. Call us later," Willa says.

"Have a good night!" Greer cheers from the door before they're gone.

"Smells good in here," my brother says, moving around the kitchen and flicking the oven light on to see what's inside.

We may not be twins, but I swear we can always sense

when the other one needs us, and his ears must have been burning.

"Hey, I'm glad you're here," I say and wave my hand for him to sit down. "Why were you and Greer having dinner together the other night?"

"You saw us?" He looks panicked.

I nod. I knew it. He likes her.

He sighs. "Grey wants to join a traveling football team next summer. Thinks he needs to change his eating habits."

I narrow my gaze at him.

"So you took him out for Mexican? Instead of just meeting at their office?"

He grabs another cookie before I can move the plate from his reach. "We were just sitting down to go over him possibly becoming a client of hers. You know, since she's a nutritionist and all."

"He's only twelve, Simon."

"Thirteen by next summer, and who am I to tell him no, you can't eat healthy?"

"True. That's all it was?"

"Yep."

I'm not so sure I believe him, but who am I kidding? Simon has no plans to settle down. He loved once, and in his mind, it won't happen again.

"There is something I need to talk to you about."

His voice is serious, and it makes me pause with the door half closed.

"Is Grey okay?"

"Grey is fine."

"Are Mom and Dad okay?"

"Everyone is fine."

"Then why do you sound like you're here to deliver bad news?"

I study him cautiously and wait for him to say something. He takes his time shrugging off his coat and running a hand through his hair, his gaze lingering around the room for a moment.

"Out with it, Simon."

"Is Beck here?"

I open my mouth to snap at him, but then close it and take a different approach. Does he know?

"No. He's making a pit stop at the store for milk on his way home. What's up?"

The longest sigh I've ever heard leaves my brother's lips, and I want to smack him.

"Simon." I all but stomp my foot.

"Alright, alright. I'm just thinking of how to say this. Give me a second."

I move the cooled cookies to a plate to make room for the ones in the oven.

"Beck asked me how I would feel if the two of you were dating."

"He did?" I spin around with a grin I can't contain.

He nods. "Yep."

"What did you say?"

Please tell me you said you'd be fine. Please be okay with it. I'd date Beck either way, but knowing my brother is okay with it makes it all the better.

"I said to take it slow."

My smile drops.

"I didn't mean it like that," my brother says softly.

"There's only one way you can say it, Simon."

"Well," he groans. "I can see that you're taking it the wrong way."

I point at him with the spatula in my hand. "Then tell me how you want me to take it."

He takes a beat before he talks.

"Beck is a romantic, okay? His whole life he's had this family who has this amazing love story: his grandparents, his parents, his sister who just got engaged. Love is important to him. Family, commitment, trust," he says slowly and waits till I look him in the eye, "is important to him."

Alright. I get what he's trying to say.

"I don't want you to break his heart. That's why I don't know if I want you to date him. Not because he's my best friend. Hell, Cals, my best friend and my sister— that would be amazing. But he'd fall for you, and I—"

"I know."

I drop into the closest seat and brush away a tear that has snuck out. Simon takes a seat next to me and puts his hand on mine.

"I'm assuming that since he asked and you smiled silly when I mentioned it, something is already going on."

I only nod.

"Does he know, then? Because I know you well enough to know that you've never had a relationship because you don't like to share this with anyone. You never talk about it."

I look up into my brother's eyes and start to cry. He pulls me into a hug and rubs his hand down my back.

"Shh, shh, it's going to be okay. I love you, Calla, and I'm not saying you two couldn't have it all together, but Cals, he needs to know everything. Sooner rather than later."

I suck in a breath and swipe the tears away.

Beck could walk through that door at any moment, and I don't need him to see me like this. I'm going to tell him. I am. But I sure as heck am not going to tell him after he's found me crying in my brother's arms.

I'm not sure if there is a right way to say it, but if there is, this isn't it.

No matter how I choose to tell him, the fact of the matter is, at the end of the day, I can't have kids. A future with me is just that. Me.

It's a big choice for someone to make, and I hate that being with me takes that choice from them.

But this is Beck. I'm falling for him. I have to tell him.

I just don't know how.

CHAPTER TWENTY-NINE
BECK

It's crazy how one day you can barely know a person, then you spend a few weeks together and suddenly, you feel like you've known them your whole life. Like you know everything about them.

I feel that with Calla. Like there was never a time in my life when I didn't know her. So right now, while we're sitting on the couch watching Wednesday on Netflix and she isn't cuddling me like she normally does, I know something is wrong. I also know that Calla isn't the kind of person to just come right out and say what's bothering her.

Still, I have to try.

"Is everything okay?" I ask, pulling her legs onto my lap and starting to rub her feet.

She nods.

Not exactly the answer I was looking for.

"Dinner was amazing," I say, and again, she nods. "Should we go get ice cream?"

"I'm still pretty full from dinner," she says, her focus never straying from her iPad.

Jeez. Earning anything other than a brush-off answer is like pulling teeth. Somewhere in the back of my mind, I know I shouldn't say more. I shouldn't keep asking her questions. If she says she's fine, she's fine. She's going to remain fine until she's ready to talk to me about whatever is on her mind.

Think, Beck, what did she do today? She woke up, we ate breakfast, and she let me kiss her. She let me touch her. She worked most of the afternoon from home. Her girls came over. Then her brother came over while she was cooking and… oh, shit. Did Simon say something to her? When I talked to him the other night, he didn't seem upset by the idea, but he was a little weird in how he responded. *Take it slow.* It felt like there was a hidden meaning behind it, but I didn't press him for obvious reasons.

Maybe she told him everything?

"How was your visit with Simon?" I ask, picking up the remote and turning the TV on to appear chill.

From the corner of my eye, I see her slowly lower the tablet and smirk at me. "How was my visit?"

I nod.

"That's a pretty formal way to ask a simple question."

"Is it?"

"Yes. You had your face between my legs not eight hours ago. Usually people on that comfort level would just ask, "What did your brother want today, or how's your brother?"

I pause to think of a response. Is it weird that she's questioning the way I stated my question? Hell, is she avoiding answering because he did, in fact, say something regarding our relationship and she doesn't want to tell me? I'm a big boy. She can tell me. Then when she's done, I'll drive myself to Simon's house and tell him all the ways that he's wrong.

I rephrase the question to move things along.

"What did your brother say today when he stopped by?" I ask and then shoot her a wink.

She giggles. "Nothing much."

"Oh."

Sweet. Good talk.

"He wanted to see if you and I have something going on," she adds nonchalantly.

I knew it!

"What did you say?"

"The truth."

"The whole truth?" I squeak out and sit up taller. "Like, all of it?"

She rolls her eyes, sets her iPad down, and curls into my side. "I left out all the sex we've been having and how you can't go a day without going down on me or how much I love to cup your—"

"I get it," I say and pinch her side. She squirms, so I take the chance to flip her on her back and then settle on top of her, nudging her knees apart with my own. "Did you tell him that we're married?"

Her nose wrinkles. "I may have left that part out too."

"Ah, so you only told him what he needed to know."

"Precisely."

I kiss her forehead.

"Are we done talking about my brother?"

Instead of waiting for an answer, she slips her hand into my sweats and wraps her fingers around me. I close my eyes as I let out a hiss. She's touched me more times than I can count in the last three weeks, and yet every time is like it's my first hit of a new drug. It's a feeling I never want to end.

I lower my hips to grind against her, which incentivizes her to remove her shirt and shimmy off her purple and white polka dot pajama shorts.

My favorite pajamas of hers.

Stripping my clothes happens just as quickly, and before we can get too carried away, we dash into the bedroom.

We make love and we cuddle, but even as I hold her in my arms while she falls asleep, something feels off.

CHAPTER THIRTY
CALLA

Beck knows something is off with me.

He's a smart man. It hasn't even been twenty-four hours since my brother dropped by, and Beck knows enough to figure out that my brother said something to upset me. I may have been able to distract him with sex last night, but I can't do it every time I see his gorgeous face and think about how the moment the words are out of my mouth, that smile I've grown to love will vanish. I'm going to hurt him, and I don't want to do it.

But I have to. The sooner the better.

Which is why I need to tell him before he brings it up to Simon and causes a fight that doesn't need to happen.

He'll be home in an hour, and I'm going to tell him.

So basically, in an hour, I'll know where we stand.

I head into Beck's office to pass the time organizing it. I bump his desk, and his computer screen lights up. In any office I've ever been in, it's common practice to lock a computer before you walk away from it, but seeing as how this is Beck's home office, it must not be something he does. Definitely not considering the document on the screen before me.

Marrying My Enemy by Beck Robertson.

Normally, I'd just look away, but the cover of an obviously new book is staring back at me. In small letters above his name it reads, an enemies-to-lovers roommates romance.

"Huh."

I sit, still looking at the screen.

That's not… that's not us. He wouldn't… he wouldn't do that.

I pull my eyes away and stand before my mind can get carried away, but then I see it. On the corner of his desk, a printout of the exact same story. It's not in a book form, just a giant stack of your typical letter-sized paper.

Curiosity gets the best of me. I move everything on the desk out of the way so that the book is the only thing in front of me.

Just one page. I'll know by one page if this is based on us. Then I'll put it back and move on with my day, feeling guilty as hell that I'm even thinking about doing this. I'll even tell Beck and we will laugh together over it.

Just one page. Maybe even just the blurb. Yes, the blurb. Perfect.

I married the woman who hates me most in this world.

I know, I know, you're wondering how that happened. Trust me, I'm just as shocked as you are, but the moral of the story is this: it happened, and there is no coming back from it.

There is no annulment or divorce—the only option we have is to make it work.

As soon as she moved in, I knew it was a bad idea. I knew that nothing good would come from this, but marriage is important to me, and I am not a person who gives up. I'll do whatever I have to do, even if that means making her fall in love with me.

I jump out of his chair like the desk had caught fire and my body was just a casualty of the blast.

He wrote about us. About me. Our… our story. He… he used me. To write a book.

My hand covers my chest, but I move it just as quickly. It feels as if there is pressure pushing against my lungs, making it hard to breathe.

"Calla, you down here?" Beck calls out, and from the sounds of it, he's jogging down the steps. "I was thinking that now that your brother knows we're dating, we should just tell him we're married and get it all out in the—whoa, whoa." He steadies me as I stumble from his office. "What's going on? Are you okay?"

All the emotions I've experienced since we got married hit me at once. Falling for Beck. Being happy that my brother isn't mad about it. Thinking we can have this life together. That I finally found the one. Worrying that my not having children could be it for us, when that's the last thing I want, then finding this book, this... this…

He pulls me to him and holds me tight, kissing the side of my head. "Whatever it is, we can work it out. Tell me what's wrong so I help fix it."

"I can't have kids," I blurt out. "You want kids, and I can't have kids."

His brows dip but smooth out quickly as he laces his hand with mine.

I start to cry harder when he hugs me once more.

"Hey, baby, it's okay." He kisses my forehead. "I'm not going anywhere. As long as—"

"Do you mean that?" I cut him off, my tears halting almost immediately as I jerk away from him.

"Yes, I do." He reaches for me, but I quickly step back.

"You're positive?"

"Yes, Calla. I'm not with you so you can have my kids, I'm with you so—"

"So that you can finish this book," I snap and toss the crumpled page in my hand at him.

For a moment, I thought he would rush to act confused, but he doesn't. He doesn't even open the paper when he catches it. Instead, his chin drops to his chest.

"It's not what you think."

"Oh, so you're not writing a book about two people who hate each other and get married?"

"No, I am, but again, it's not what you think."

"Is it based off us?"

His face wrinkles.

"I knew it."

"Hey, the premise is us, yes, but what the characters do is not. It's fiction, Calla. It started as a way for me to vent, and then my agent saw it. I told him no, but the offers were too good to be true, and it's not us, okay? Like us, but not."

"So the heroine doesn't try to sabotage the hero?"

"Fuck. Okay, a little, but—"

"God." I step back from him. "Oh my god."

"Calla, just hear me out, please."

"Was any of this real?"

"All of it. Every single day."

"How am I supposed to believe you? This hero," I point to his computer, "tricks her into staying married to help his writing career. Is that what you're doing? Was the whole 'my family believes in marriage' the truth or a sack of shit to fool me?"

"It's the truth, I swear."

"And you never once thought that divorce would hurt your image?"

He closes his eyes and drops his chin to his chest again.

"Fucking hell, Beck."

"Of course I thought of it, Calla. I am my own brand, but this book was never the reason I wanted to stay married to you."

"So your reputation *is* the only reason you want to stay married?"

"It was at first. Now—"

"Now I have no idea what to believe. You literally make shit up for a living. How am I supposed to believe you?"

"Calla," he says slowly and reaches for me.

"Don't."

"Please just… fuck, I wanted to tell you, but there was never a good time."

"Never a good time to be honest? Ha. Wow. Every moment we spend together is a great moment to be honest with me."

"Like you were honest with me?" His voice is laced with sarcasm. "Clearly, we don't tell each other everything."

Oh, the nerve.

"Do not turn this on me because you fucked up."

His eyes close again, and he lets out a breath.

"You're right. I screwed up. Let's just," he waves toward the stairs, "let's just go get some air and talk about this."

I nod. "You should go get some air. I'd like to be alone anyway. I need to think."

"Calla, I don't want to end this conversation like this. I don't want to leave this unresolved, okay? I'm in—"

"Well, I want you to not use our personal life as the basis of your next bestseller. Now, please, let me have some space."

He stumbles back but nods.

"Fine, but we are not going to bed fighting. Do you hear me? I will be back, and we will fix this."

I shake my head and turn toward my room.

"I'm going to Tobias's. Call me when you want me to come back. If not, I'll be home by dinner."

I don't have a reply as I close my door.

The tears break instantly, and my vision falls blurry as I send a text to the writers' girls group—yep, I named us because I thought... it doesn't matter anymore. I know I told Beck I want to be alone, but it's not really true. I just need to not be around him.

The longer I stood there, the more I wanted to forgive him, but the fact of the matter is, he used me to write a book. Okay, yeah, maybe it didn't start that way, but he kept doing it even after we started a real relationship, and he never told me.

Fuck.

I curl up on my bed once Greer, Nora, and Natalie reply they're on the way over.

I kept a secret from him, too, but my secret didn't involve using our lives and our feelings to make a buck.

I don't know what to think.

My shoulders shake as I cry.

Beck was supposed to be the one guy who would never hurt me.

And he just did.

CHAPTER THIRTY-ONE

BECK

Before I back out of the driveway, I shoot Tobias a quick text to let him know I'm headed his way.

What the hell is wrong with me?

How did I let this happen?

I'm a smart man, a wise one. Why the hell didn't I just tell her? She was absolutely right when she said that every moment together was the perfect moment to tell her.

And fuck, she can't have kids?

All I wanted to do was kiss her and hug her when she said those words.

Telling me clearly took its toll on her, and she was obviously struggling to share her situation. Then she found my book, and fuck. How can I be there for her when I'm causing her pain?

Actually, fuck this.

I pause at the stop sign.

I need to go back. I need to fight for her. I need to show

her how wrong I was and how sorry I am and that kids or not, she's the one I want.

I turn my blinker on and flip around, barely making out the front of a truck to my left before everything goes black.

CHAPTER THIRTY-TWO
CALLA

"Can I get you anything?"

It's the tenth time one of them has asked me this question. All the girls showed up, and I gave them a quick rundown of what happened. Since then, I haven't stopped crying.

My phone rings from the nightstand, so I reach out and silence the call.

"Maybe that's him," Nora says quietly.

"I don't want to talk to him," I say on a deep breath. "Not yet."

"That's just fine." Willa rubs my back. "If he's as crazy about you as I think he is, he will wait."

"I just… why? I can't understand why he wouldn't tell me. I mean, was he waiting to see how we played out, was it just inspiration for the story? He's a writer, for heaven's sake. What if none of it was real?"

"That's not possible," Natalie says.

"We don't know that."

"Yeah, but he—"

My phone rings again.

I silence it, but Nora grabs it and hands it to me. "Just answer it. He'll keep calling if you don't."

She's probably right.

But there's an unknown number on the screen.

"It's not him," I say and let out the breath I'd been holding.

"Answer it anyway—maybe that's who keeps calling."

I nod. "Hello?"

"Hi, is this Calla Robertson?"

I scoff at the name that rolls off the woman's lips.

"Yeah, sure."

"Calla, this is Officer Flores. Your husband has been in an accident and was just checked into Wind Valley Medical Center. He was conscious just long enough to provide us with your name and number. The second car hit his driver side, and his head was..."

The rest of her words turn into a *whomp, whomp* Charlie Brown teacher noise. Heat creeps up my neck and spreads through my body. Everything starts to shake, and my heart beats swiftly.

"What?" I ask, cutting her off as I jump up, covering my mouth with a wobbly hand. The tears return on cue. "He what?"

"He's there now. You can check in at the main office, and they will direct you when you get here."

"Get where?" I ask, and it feels like a silly question but I... I'm not sure I understand.

This isn't real."

"To the hospital. Ma'am, are you okay to drive?"

"Yes."

"Perfect, someone will be expecting you."

The call ends, but I just stand here, frozen with the phone to my ear. The girls surround me, and I see their lips moving but hear nothing.

Beck was in an accident. He's not conscious. Is he in surgery? And the last...

I gasp, cupping both cheeks with my hands. The last conversation we had was a fight.

"He said he'd be back." Everyone stops talking. "He said he'd be back, and now he's in the hospital, and I don't even know if he's awake, and I need to go and what if he—" I break into sobs. Someone hugs me.

"Let's get going."

"I'll call Hero."

"I'll call Zane."

"I'll call your brother."

"He said he'll be back," I repeat, then as if someone slapped me, igniting the adrenaline, I pull myself together and run up the stairs to my car.

I break a lot of rules driving to the emergency room. Greer never says a word when a light turns yellow, and my foot turns to lead.

I've never been driven, pun intended, to get somewhere as quickly as possible. Beck left because of me. Because I was upset and wanted him to leave. All because I didn't believe him over a book.

This isn't what should've happened.

I pull up to the doors and put the car in park.

"I'll park your car and meet you inside," Greer says, rushing around the hood to take my spot.

"Thank you."

"Your brother is here already, just FYI. He's waiting for you," Greer adds before she pulls away.

How did he make it here so fast?

The doors slide open, and the smell of bleach and fear surround me. I take a breath to pull myself together and look at the directory so I know where to go. Once I find my floor, I head for the elevator. Sure enough, Simon is right there when I get off.

"Calla, hey, they won't tell me anything," he rushes to say. "I called his sister and parents, but they're in Melody and will be another hour, and the doctor and nurses won't let me see him, and they won't let me do anything and he's my best friend and I just—" His head falls into his hands as he drops into the closest chair. "I can't do anything."

If I'm scared, then Simon is tenfold. Having lost Grey's mom to a car wreck, I can't imagine the way he's feeling right now. I pat his back and take another breath. I need to be strong for him and for Beck.

"I know you said they didn't tell you much, but what did they say?"

"That they can't tell me anything because I'm not family."

Ah. Well, I suppose this is where I come in.

"Oh, there's the doctor. Excuse me, doctor," Simon says and rushes to stop him.

I follow right behind my brother.

A pained expression covers the man's face. "I'm sorry, sir. I can't tell you anything unless you are immediate family."

"I'm his wife," I blurt out, and Simon's neck basically snaps to look at me.

The doctor flips a page on his chart.

"What's your name?"

"Calla Robertson."

The doctor nods and gives me a tight smile.

"I can walk you back to see him."

"Thank you. Is my brother allowed to come with me?" I nod toward Simon.

"Of course. Follow me."

Simon doesn't say anything; he just grabs my hands and squeezes it tight. I know he's going to have a million questions for me later, and later is just fine. The most important thing we need to do right now is see Beck.

I pause at the door the doctor informs us belongs to Beck.

"The good news is, outside of a few broken ribs, a dislocated shoulder, and more bruises than one cares to count, no surgery was required. I'll give you three a moment before I return to fill you in on more and discuss the recovery time."

I don't stop the tears, tugging Simon back when he starts to enter.

"Hold on," I say, and the doctor steps away to give us some privacy. "I... I..."

"He's going to be fine, Calla. Let's go see our boy, alright? Everything else can wait."

I nod.

The room is dark; only a little light from behind the curtain is peeking through. It glows over Beck's face, which is covered in bruises and scratches. It looks like one eye is swollen and one arm is wrapped in a sling.

Simon clears his throat, which causes Beck to open his eyes. Well, eye, because I was right— one is swollen shut.

"Hi," I say first.

Beck doesn't say anything. He just lets out a breath and closes his eyes.

It's at this moment I realize that the book doesn't matter to me. I believe him. He'd never do anything to hurt me.

"How ya feeling, buddy?" Simon asks.

"Like shit," Beck answers with a scratchy voice. I grab the water from his bedside table and help him sip.

"Thanks."

"No problem."

Silence fills the room, and yet my head is swarming with the conversations that should be happening right now.

"So, uh, you married my sister?" Simon asks, smiling at Beck.

Beck's eyes flash to mine.

"They wouldn't let us in unless we were immediate family."

"Oh," Simon says. "Sneaky. I thought it was real."

"It is," Beck and I respond at the same time.

I'm sure, all things considered right now, keeping secrets isn't the right choice anymore.

My brother must sense the tension because he backs up.

"I'll give you two a minute. I'm glad you're okay, man. I better go call Grey and his babysitter."

The room returns to its silence.

I have so much to say but now isn't the place. I still need time to think, and being away from him will help me do that, but I also can't leave him on his own.

"I'm not moving out yet," I tell him and sit next to his bed. I reach for him but stop myself, opting to just pat the bed next to him. "I'll stay to help you, but once you're healed and can take care of yourself, I'll move into my own place," I say, cutting to the chase.

"You don't have to do that."

"No, but I want to."

"Do you really?"

I can't look at him. *No, not really.* But his entire life was almost taken from him today. If I stay, I take the future he's dreamed about with a family.

"I'm not just going to leave you to fend for yourself, Beck."

"I have a family who can crash with me for a bit. I don't want you to feel forced into anything."

"I know you don't, but I'm already living there, and even if I didn't stay, I wouldn't be out of my room right away. Whoever is helping you will know that I live there and ask questions. Right now, there are more important things to focus on."

He coughs, so I grab the water and ice chips and help him take another small sip.

"I'll do exactly as the doctor says so that you don't have to be there any longer than necessary."

I nod. "Thank you."

"For what it's worth," he says quietly, "I'm sorry I hurt you."

I swallow hard and look away to keep the tears from falling. He deserves better than this.

"Okay, so I got apple juice and chocolate muffins," Simon says, joining us at the perfect moment.

"Aww, look at you two. The newlyweds are happy to be reunited."

I cringe.

"Can you not tell my family that we're married?" Beck asks once Simon is seated.

"What? Why?"

"Because," I interrupt, "it…" My words trail off as I look at Beck.

"Calla and I are still trying to figure things out, since it all moved so quickly," he says, and I nod.

He's not wrong, and this answer definitely detours my brother from asking a lot more questions.

"I still can't believe you're married," Simon says with a grin. "My best friend and my sister, This is fucking awesome. Now you're my family for real."

Simon's beam is like a staple gun to my heart. His expression right now is exactly why we didn't want to tell Beck's family. Watching people we love be thrilled for us while we, or I, know it won't last—it hurts. I could just tell my brother the entire truth right now, but today has already been a bit of an emotional rollercoaster for all of us. I'll tell him later once Beck is home and settled and resting.

And once he's good to go, I'll be on my way.

CHAPTER THIRTY-THREE
BECK

I feel like I've been hit by a bus.

It was a delivery truck, but all the same. My body feels like it's five hundred pounds, and moving on my own is almost impossible. Thank god I have one hand mobile to do the basic things, but still, here I am, trying to get out of bed so I can take a piss, and twisting to get both feet on the floor is painful as hell. The sting is so bad I feel like I could puke.

"Fuck," I growl out, and Calla is in my doorway in seconds.

"What are you doing?" she asks and rushes to me. She squats in front of me to move my legs, and it takes all my strength not to get aroused at the position she's in. Sex or anything close should be the last thing on my mind, but this is Calla. Her body was made for me and mine for her.

"You shouldn't be doing this on your own," she says softly.

"I can do some things on my own."

"Okay." She stands. I try to do the same, but I sink back into the mattress once she backs up. "Show me."

I let out a sigh and then take a deep breath, pushing off the bed with all my might. A sharp pain zips through my entire body, and I sit back down. Truth be told, I'm not even sure my ass even left the sheets. It sure felt like I jumped though.

"I told you," Calla says, sitting next to me and hooking my good arm around her shoulders. "On the count of three, okay?"

"Yeah."

"One, two, three!"

"Fuck, fuck. Fuck." I let out a breath. I am indeed standing now. "Thank you."

"Yep. Where are we headed?"

"The bathroom."

"Alright."

Without one single complaint—she hasn't complained since I got home two days ago—Calla walks at a snail's pace by my side. Once we reach the bathroom, she dips out from under my arm. "I'll just be right outside the door, unless... you know, you'll be a minute. I can grab your phone for you so you can text me. I don't want to be weird and stand outside the door while you're doing... that."

I chuckle and then wince. "I'm not doing that. I just need to pee and then take a shower."

"You can't shower."

"I can shower."

She steps back into the bathroom and crosses her arms. I swear her eyes get brighter as she tilts her head. "No, that's standing for too long and although your legs aren't broken, your body has been through enough. You can take a bath."

"I'm not taking a bath. I'm not a bath kind of guy."

"You were that one night with me." She looks away quickly, biting her bottom lip.

"Are you offering to take one with me? If so, then yeah, I'm a bath guy."

"No, I'm not."

"Then no bath."

"Beck," she snaps, "the doctor said no showers for the first week. Baths only, so unless you are going to delay your healing process, then I suggest you do as you're told. Go pee. I'll be back to draw you a bath."

"Draw me a bath." I laugh.

"Beck," she says once more, firmly.

Now, I'm not sure if it's the painkillers or because even though my main focus should be on getting better, all I can think about is how I hurt her and yet she's still here for me, but as soon as I open my mouth to mention it, her eyes capture me, and I swear they say *please. Please don't do this to us.*

I simply nod, and then she's out the door.

I call for her when I'm done, and she does exactly what she said and starts a bath.

She helps me into the warm water and then leaves me to my thoughts. They are of her, of course. I should have pushed harder to have my mother or sister stay with me. Having Calla so close but still so far away hurts worse than my entire body.

I sit until the water turns cold.

What can I say to Calla to make this better? I miss her. My bed feels wrong without her. My life feels wrong now that I know she'll soon be out of it. I don't want her to go. I want to make this better.

"Beck, is everything okay?" She pokes her head in the door.

"Yeah, I'm ready to get out."

I feel like a toddler asking my mom to get my towel, but I watch Calla's every move, and she doesn't even try to sneak a peek. She's fully respectable, and I want her not to be.

I dry off and get dressed, hobbling to the bed with her help.

"I'm sorry about the book," I say in almost a whisper. "I'm going to tell Doug to pull all the contracts for the books and the movies."

She doesn't say anything as she straightens my sheets.

"I should have talked to you first. I'm so sorry, Calla."

Still nothing as she opens one of my prescription bottles and sets two pills next to my water.

"Please, say something."

"You need to take these in an hour."

"Not about that."

She takes a deep breath. "Don't pull the book, Beck."

I let out a huff of a chuckle. "I can't let them release it now. Every time someone reviews it, I'll be reminded of how I hurt you and how—"

"Our story didn't hurt me, Beck. You did. Not telling me about it hurt."

My heart stings.

"But I forgive you, okay? Now, get some rest."

She forgives me. Is that a sign that we can get past this?

"Will you stay with me?" I look up to gauge her reaction. She was already leaning over to adjust the pillow behind my head when the words left my mouth.

She pauses mid-fluff.

"I just… I miss you, and I assume I'll need help during the night. It would be nice just to know you're here."

I don't know why I can't outright tell her to stay because I want her to and because she wants to. A lot has happened in the past few days—maybe I don't want to rush her. Just because she's forgiven me doesn't mean we can go back to how things were.

"Are you sure this isn't just an excuse to get me to stay with you because you want me close?"

"Not completely."

She lets out a long sigh. "Well, at least you're honest now."

Ouch.

She makes a show of looking at her watch and then the door. I'm not sure why, but she looks back at me slowly.

"I can easily just wake you up when it's time for your medicine, and I'm a text or call away. I don't need to be in here the entire night."

"Please, Calla."

"Beck, don't do this to me, please."

Her pleading tone breaks me, and the last thing I want to do is make her hurt again.

"Alright. Good night, Calla."

"Good night," she says and hightails it from my room.

For the next ten days, I try to talk to her every chance I get, but she evades every topic. The book, kids, marriage… all of it.

All the things we clearly need to talk about.

For once in my life, I might not have the words to fix this.

CHAPTER THIRTY-FOUR
CALLA

"I don't know what I'm doing," I confess as soon as the door to my room is closed. Yep, I'm back in the basement. Which makes sense, but everything about it feels wrong.

"Okay, we'll circle back to what you're doing after you tell us how you're doing," Greer says. She starts unloading a bag of snacks and drinks. It's nothing healthy. Cookies and chips and dip and black cherry Fresca.

"I don't even know how to answer that." I grab the package of Chewy Chips Ahoy and then spot the red velvet Oreos and grab that instead. I jerk the back open, ripping it down the middle, and chomp on a cookie. With a mouthful, I say, "Fine. I think."

"Yeah, I don't believe you." Willa steals a cookie for herself. She glances at the broken-down boxes and packing tape that sits on top of them, but she doesn't say a word.

"I don't either." I close my eyes on a sigh and lean against my headboard. Then I burst into tears.

"Hey, it's okay," Greer says, coming to my side and rubbing my back.

"Don't cry, hun, everything is okay," Willa adds.

"I know." I take a breath. "And Beck is going to be just fine, but I… what if that had been our last conversation? What if he hadn't been okay?"

The days have been long since Beck came home from the hospital. After I told him that I forgave him about the book, he never mentioned it again. He's tried to bring up the kids thing and me not moving out, but I've shut him down every single time.

There isn't much to say.

If we stay together, I take away his dream for kids. I care about his future. The future we were both so easily reminded can be taken from us at any moment. No matter what he says, he's a mix of emotions and painkillers right now, and he's clinging to the idea of me. That's all. He's just living on that "I almost died and should live life to the fullest" high. He isn't thinking clearly.

He thinks he'll be happy with just the two of us.

"Stop, you can't think like that. I know it's hard, but you have to try. He's fine. You're fine. He's home."

The sobs rack through me, and my friend just lets me cry. It's like they sense that I need to let it out.

"This might not be the right time to ask this, but are you two still planning on splitting up?"

I nod.

"But," Greer hesitates, "is that still what you want?"

Do I want to leave? No, not really.

"I don't think it matters what I want anymore. He wants…" I stammer.

Aside from my family, no one knows that kids aren't an option for me. Beck wants kids. I can't give him kids. Me leaving just makes sense. Finding that book was a sign that I need to get out before it's too late. It's like the universe wanted me to see it before I put myself through something it knew I couldn't come back from.

"It very much so matters, Calla."

"I can't have kids," I say so quietly that I'm almost worried I didn't actually say it.

When I look up at my friends, though, both have expressions that are a mix of pain and sadness. Knowing them, they won't ask questions, but maybe talking about it will help.

"When I was in high school, I had abnormal bleeding so bad and so frequently that I was admitted to the hospital multiple times. Eventually, a hysterectomy was the best option to keep me safe."

Greer's hand goes to her mouth while a tear slips down Willa's cheek.

"Beck wants kids, and I can't." I don't even get the words out before I'm shaking my head and crying right along with them.

"Does he know?" Willa asks.

"Yes, but we haven't talked about it. I was so mad when I found the book that I just blurted it out. We argued. He left, the accident happened, and it doesn't even matter."

"It does though."

"Why?"

"He still wants to be with you," Greer says.

"Yes, he does," Willa whispers. "You can see it every single time he looks at you."

My mind wanders to all the moments Beck and I have had

this week. All the times I've caught him watching me. All the times he's tried to make conversation with me over these things and I changed the subject. The result, no matter how much we discuss it, is that we shouldn't be together.

"Do you want to talk about this right now?" Willa asks.

"Not really. Quick, someone change the subject. Make me laugh."

"Zane let me paint his toes the other night," Willa says at the same time Greer says, "I caught Matt cheating on me, so I cut the crotch out of all his underwear."

The three of us exchange looks and then burst into laughter.

"Thank you."

"Anytime," Greer says.

I take a deep breath before I speak again. "The choice of whether I can have kids was taken from me. I don't want to take the choice from someone else. That's exactly what I'd be doing if I let Beck stay married to me."

"Understandable." Greer nods. "But you should talk it over with Beck and let him make that choice."

"That's just it." I groan. "I know he'll pick me."

Even though I forgave him, letting him believe this book thing is why I'm leaving is easier than the truth. The truth is complicated.

"So that's the problem?" Willa asks.

"The problem is that I let him fall for me before I told him, so it feels like I already took it. The best thing for me to do is leave."

"Is that what's best for him or what's best for you?" Willa asks.

"Both?"

Both friends give me sad smiles as we eat our snacks.

I let out a big sigh. I don't know what else to say.

"Should we start the new season of *Ginny and Georgia*?" Greer asks.

Willa and I agree, but even as we sit in silence to watch the show, my mind is racing with what they asked me.

Is my leaving what's best for him or what's best for me?

CHAPTER THIRTY-FIVE
CALLA

When you live with someone long enough, you memorize their habits and start to predict their next move. The way he lingers in my doorway, pretending to look at the trim, I know he's pumping himself up to ask me something he knows I don't want to talk about.

That can be only one thing right now.

Beck.

"Your hovering is putting me on edge. What do you want to say?" I blurt out as I check under the bed to make sure I didn't forget anything.

Besides the box by my brother's feet, everything of mine has been moved out of Beck's house and into either my car or my brother's.

"I think you might be making a mistake by leaving."

"I told you what happened, Simon."

"You also said you forgave him, so what's the problem?"

I roll my eyes and start to move past him.

"He didn't die, Calla. He's right here. Don't freak out because of what could have happened."

"That's not it, trust me, Simon."

"He makes you hap—"

"Can we not have this conversation now? I need to go. Get away from this house and think, Simon. Please, just help me do that."

Just because I'm leaving doesn't mean I'm emotionally ready to let Beck go. Getting away to think may sound silly, but it's what I need.

I swipe a tear off my cheek, and he nods.

"Okay, yeah, let's go."

We make it up the stairs and out the door before Beck catches up to us. I thought I could be faster than him with his leg.

"Calla," he says softly behind me. "Please don't go."

I motion for Simon to go to the car without me.

As soon as I turn around, Beck gets right to it.

"Don't leave, Calla." He kisses my forehead. "I can't do this without you. I don't want to do this without you."

I hitch my next breath as I hold in the urge to cry.

"We aren't meant to be together, Beck."

"Yes, we are."

I shake my head.

"Baby, come on, we are." His pleading almost does me in.

"We just… we want different things."

"Do we?" he asks. "Because I'm pretty sure we both want to be together. You're just being stubborn as hell right now."

"Well, that's the winning line to get me to stay," I say with heavy sarcasm.

I turn to walk away, but he stops me.

"If this is about the kids thing, that doesn't matter to me, Calla. You matter to me. Us."

The soft expression in his eyes as he looks into my own makes me want to believe him, but I've had years to accept this. He hasn't.

"You've known for two weeks, Beck. You need to take time to think about it and process and—"

"I don't need to take any time to process that I want to be with you."

"Beck, so much has happened recently. With the accident, I think maybe you're making decisions because you're scared that life is short."

"I'm not scared, Calla. Come on. Don't run like you did in Vegas. Talk to me. Stay. Let's make this work."

"I'm not running this time, Beck. I'm standing right here, telling you that we aren't meant to be together."

"I don't agree with you, so I'm going to need more than that."

"Beck, please stop."

"Tell me exactly why we shouldn't be together, and I'll stop."

"Because!" I whirl around and shout. I don't get another word out before tears spill over my cheeks.

Immediately, Beck reaches for my hands.

"Okay, okay," he starts, wiping away as many tears as he can. "Go to your brother's and call me later. We can finish this after we have both had a moment to breathe. I don't want one of us saying something we don't mean."

He kisses my forehead again, and then I turn for the car, all the while knowing that I won't call him later.

CHAPTER THIRTY-SIX
BECK

I'm going to be sick.

If it isn't from the fact that Calla still hasn't called me, it's because of the papers sitting on my passenger seat.

Divorce papers.

Not signed, to be clear. I didn't sign them, but I got them. For her. Because as far as I know that's still what she wants. I just want her to be happy. I'll do anything, even this, if that's what it takes.

To be even more clear, it's not what I want. Not even close.

I just have no idea how to reach her. To talk to her. She won't answer my calls, and she won't send messages back through her brother. Yes, that's how desperate I've been to contact her. It's been the longest two weeks of my life.

Big fat silence is all I've got. I could wait, give her more time, but if I can't get through to her now, I never will.

So, yeah, the papers are my last-ditch effort to communicate.

I glance over at the manilla envelope that haunts me and then to the smaller white one on top. The one that has an application for a new driver's license. For her birthday, I'd added her name to all the bills for the house. Nothing was ready on her actual birthday, but she'd need proof to get a new license with her new address and new last name. I even filled out everything on the application for her. All she needs to do is sign it. It was a silly way for me to re-propose, I guess.

Heat creeps up my neck. I'm about to give her both things and pray to god she picks the application.

Picks us.

I pull into Simon's driveaway, and the door opens before I make it up the walkway.

"Hey," I say and Calla sighs, leaning into the doorway. "I know you don't want to see me, but I"—fuck, this is hard—"I…"

I can't bring myself to say the words, so I hold up the folder.

"Oh," she says. "Do you want to come in?"

"Yes," I say before she can change her mind.

I follow her into the kitchen. Every cabinet and every drawer is open, and all the plates, cups, dry food, and more cover the counters.

"I'm reorganizing Simon's kitchen. It was horrendous."

"Yeah, I believe it. He mentioned that you signed that contract with the real estate agent. That's great."

"Thanks. Do you want anything to drink?" she asks. Her tone is light, and everything is the opposite from when I spoke with her last. Maybe, just maybe, this is my chance. Only one way to find out.

"Yeah, water is great. Are you baking too?"

"I am," she says and glances at the stove. "The first batch is almost done."

I move closer to her and grab a spoon that's on display. Then I swipe a scoop of dough. I've barely put it in my mouth before she swats my hand away and steals the spoon.

"Don't," she says and then looks at the bowl. She does exactly as I did. "Great, now I won't be able to stop."

I chuckle and she smiles, her eyes drifting to the bigger envelope.

"You don't have to sign it," I say, skipping right to the point. "We don't have to do this. We can stay married and fix this. I can fix this. I know I messed up by keeping things from you, but I… need you. I want you in my life, Calla. Forever."

"Beck, I—"

"Don't say anything right now, okay? I don't want you to feel like you have to decide right here and right now because I'm standing in front of you confessing my love to you. I love you so much, Calla, it hurts when you aren't near me. I only ask that you just think about it."

She takes a deep breath and lets it out slowly.

I set the large yellow envelope with the divorce papers down, followed by one with the application, and finally a smaller one, the one that has the letter I wrote her. I'll say what I need to say before I walk out her door, but words and paper are really where I do my best work.

"All these envelopes mean something. I love you more than anything in this world, Calla, but I want you to choose us because that's what you want. Not because we signed some papers one night in Vegas. I can't promise I won't mess up again, but I want that chance because being without you is like knowing I'll never eat again. It hurts like hell.

"The biggest envelope is the obvious but promise me you'll look at the other one before you sign those papers. You might not feel like what happened between us was right, but I can assure you, Calla, marrying you that night in Vegas was the right choice. Let me prove it to you."

She started crying somewhere during my confession, but she never moved away from me. The urge to pull her close is strong, but I'm not sure if that's—fuck it. I wrap my arms around her shoulders and hold her tight.

"I didn't come here with the intention of making you cry, baby, I swear it. I only wanted to make sure you know exactly where I stand."

"I know, I just... I don't know where I stand."

I kiss the top of her head. "That's okay. Just don't do anything until you know. That's all I ask."

"But there are so many obstacles that prove we shouldn't be together."

"The only obstacle I see is how to get you back home as quickly as possible."

She chokes up and steps out of my reach.

"I need more time."

"Okay, take all the time you need. Take a day, two days, a month, a year even. Whenever you're ready, I will be here. I'll wait as long as you need me to."

"That's not fair to you."

"When it's for the woman I love, it's more than fair."

I can see that the waterworks are about to begin again, so I step back.

"You know where to find me."

"I do."

I open the door, pausing before I leave. With one last look over my shoulder, I say. "I love you, Calla."

And I walk out the door. I leave the ball in her court. I've done all that I can do, and now I just have to wait and see if she'll choose me.

CHAPTER THIRTY-SEVEN
CALLA

Before I was a teenager, I remember sneaking out of my room once my parents thought I was asleep and sitting at the top of the steps, listening to them reminisce about the day. They'd talk about what happened at work, and then they would talk about me and Simon. They'd share what they each saw us do that day that made them the most proud and mention how lucky they were to have such great children. I remember thinking, "Wow, this is what I want."

Yeah, I was young, but I knew even back then that I wanted to be a wife and mom. It was a package deal.

A package deal that I dreamed about every single day until that dream was taken from me.

Then I married Beck.

Then I left Beck.

Then I learned that I already had those kinds of moments. The moments where it doesn't matter what you're talking about, it just matters who you're talking with.

Beck is my person. These past couple of weeks have shown me that. I thought getting away from him would help me move on, but it did the opposite. It showed me how much I love him.

It's just … I can't seem to let go of the guilt of what being with me means.

"Are you going to open the letter?" Greer asks, pouring me a glass of wine and one for herself. Simon takes the seat next to her and picks it up.

"I can't believe it's been here for a whole day, and you haven't opened it. Beck is probably at home just dying."

"He's not dying. Upset, yes, and planning his next move to show up here, I'm sure, but dying? No. He would be fine without me."

"So that's your choice?" Greer asks.

"I don't agree with you, and even if I did, would you be okay without him?" Simon adds his own line of questioning.

Of course not. He's my person. There will never be another man in my life like Beck.

I don't answer either of them. Instead, I slide the letter toward myself and stare at it.

If I could have kids, yes, I'd be with Beck in a heartbeat. I'd be clinging to him every chance I got to give us everything we want.

It just doesn't feel right to think it can still be that easy. To not feel guilty.

It isn't that I don't want to read the letter; I'm beside myself with the fact that I haven't yet. I'm certain that whatever is in this letter is going to make me choose Beck, and yes, that's all well and dandy, but this isn't a light choice to make. It's a good thing he isn't here. No words or his smile or his perfect scent to influence me. Most of all, not his touch. Simply being near that man can make every inch of my body relax into a state where I'd agree to anything he wanted.

I know he said it didn't matter to him, but one day it might. And deep down, I'll always feel like it's my fault he isn't getting everything he wants in life. By choosing him and choosing us, it feels selfish.

But the longer I string this out, the longer we both hurt.

Today is the day I make a decision. Either I'll choose to believe that I'm enough for him or I need to let him go.

On a breath, I pull out the letter.

Dear Calla,

Let me preface this letter by telling you once again how much I love you. Neither of us expected this to happen after we got married, but I wholeheartedly believe that we walked down that aisle for a reason. We might not have known what it was that night, but there was a reason.

Mine was because I kept spending all this time searching for the perfect woman when she was right here the whole time. I was too blind to see how perfect you are for me. I was too blind to see how you make me smile as soon as I wake up. You make me want to be better and do better; you make me want to try new things and take chances I never would have before. You are the missing piece of my life, and I'm so sorry that I hurt you. That I didn't tell you the truth. That you couldn't trust me to be honest.

I was scared the truth would ruin what we had, but the only person who did that was me.

You are the only person I want to share the good and the

bad with, and I hope to god you will give me a chance to be that man for you. To be someone you trust and want to spend your life with. If you do, please start by trusting me when I say, YOU are the most important person in my life and YOU are the only future I want and need.

I love you, Calla Robertson. Please come home.

Love, your husband.

I fold the letter and gently put it back, tears spilling down my cheeks.

I close my eyes until I've pulled myself together.

I have to trust him. I have to believe him.

"You know what? Fine, here." Simon opens the white envelope, jerks out the papers. "Sign these and be done with it. You're not the only one hurting, Calla. That man loves you. Sign these papers and be done with him. You don't call him. You don't text him. You don't hug or kiss him or whatever. You're done."

A sickening feeling forms in my stomach.

Never see Beck again?

"Jesus, Simon. You don't have to be so harsh." Greer smacks his shoulder.

"Someone has to tell her how it is."

My gaze falls to the papers, and I see it instantly.

A smile spreads across my lips.

"These aren't divorce papers," I say.

"No shit, Sherlock," Simon says. "He doesn't want to divorce you."

"Yeah, but he—"

Screw this. These two are not who I need to have this conversion with.

I grab the papers, the letter, and the big envelope still unopened off the table and shove them into my purse.

I grab my coat and am halfway out the door as Simon yells, "Don't come back! You can't live here anymore!"

If all goes as planned, I won't need to.

I hop in my car, simultaneously backing up and tugging on my seat belt.

I'm such a fool for waiting this long.

I pull into his driveway and I'm halfway up the front walk when he opens the door.

I don't get any words out. I don't do anything but smile at him. Then I run.

He catches me when I leap, wobbling a bit because I'm sure his body is still sore, but he wraps his arms around me as if he'll never let go.

I sure as hell hope he doesn't.

"I'm sorry," I say as he lowers me back to my feet. "I'm so sorry it took me this long to figure it out."

"Baby, as long as your choice is us, I don't care how long it took you."

"I love you."

"I love you too."

Then I flick his chest.

"Ouch."

"That's for making me think you signed divorce papers."

He chuckles and wrinkles his nose.

"Technically, I never said I signed then, just that I got them."

"So then what is this?" I hold up the driver's license application. "Looks like you put a lot more effort into completing this one."

"Yeah, well, I wanted that one more. All you have to do is sign it and put it in the mail. I think it takes only a few weeks to get a new driver's license. You'll officially be Calla Robertson."

I shake my head and let out a huff.

"If we're going to make this work, we both have to agree to be honest about everything no matter how scared we might be to tell the other one."

"Deal." He kisses my forehead.

"So… you should know that I didn't leave because of all the book stuff."

"Yeah, I had a feeling it wasn't."

I lick my lips and bite my lip as I struggle to find my words. "I…"

"I love you," he says, a finger to my chin guiding my gaze to his. "I love everything about you, and I can't wait to spend the rest of my life with you."

I nod quickly. The guilt and worry over whether or not he'll be happy with just me is replaced with more love than I've ever felt.

I hate to admit that we could have resolved this weeks ago if I had just talked to him, but sometimes, you have to make a few wrong choices to make the right choice.

That's just life.

I push him back with my hands on his chest. "There are more things you should know," I tell him. And because teasing each other is what we do best, I let him sweat it for a good twenty seconds.

"I want a dog," I say.

He grins and nods.

"A big dog. Like a lab."

"Okay."

"No cats."

"Noted."

"And I want a firepit in the backyard and planters under the windows and one of the walls in the basement needs to be built-in bookshelves and—"

"Can I ask a question yet?" he cuts me off, leaning in to press his lips softly at the nape of my neck.

My heart swells, and the thought of where those lips will be in the next ten minutes consumes me.

"It better be a good one."

"Oh, it is." He winks and kneels. "Calla Robertson, will you marry me, again?"

He pops open a ring box, and a square-cut diamond shines up at me.

"Have you just been carrying this around?"

He laughs. "I've had pretty high hopes for the last twenty-four hours."

"I'll say." I drop to my knees to join him on the cement and nibble at his bottom lip. "Yes."

He wraps his arms around my waist, standing as he peppers kisses from my lips to my neck and back to my mouth.

"I knew it. I knew it all along," he says when I wrap my legs around his hips.

"Knew what?"

"That marrying you was one of my best decisions."

"Do you know what else is a good decision?"

"What?"

"Taking me inside. Right. Now."

His only answer is a growl as he does just that.

Being happy is risky, but at the end of that day, Beck isn't wrong.

Getting married was definitely the right choice.

EPILOGUE
GRAHAM

The grin on my face is starting to hurt my cheeks. Good things are happening to everyone around me.

"Is this for real?" Zane asks, his eyes giant saucers and his arms folded in front of him.

"Real as it gets," Hero says, a proud smile on his face as his gaze never leaves the picture in his hand.

A sonogram, for him and Nora.

"And now is when you wanted to share it with the group?" Zane asks.

"Yep." Hero laughs. "It was now or in thirty minutes and steal the thunder from your fresh engagement."

"Shhh!" Zane flails his hands around and pins each of us with a glare. Our entire group is here tonight for this: me, Hero, Beck, Simon, Tobias, and, of course, Zane. He is, after all, one-half of the main event.

When Zane is confident the coast is clear, he faces Hero with a shit-eating grin.

"Congrats, man," he says, going in for a hug and single back pat.

The rest of us follow suit but then fall silent as Zane shuffles his feet and focuses on the doors.

In about five minutes, Willa is going to meet us all down here for just dinner, or so she thinks, and he's going to drop to his knee and ask her to spend forever with him.

We're back at Lovers Lodge for the weekend. Zane claims that since this is the place he fell in love with Willa, it only makes sense to do this here.

That'll officially make three of my best friends married off. The romance addict inside me is here for this, and I support each of them no matter how we got here.

Willa, of course, thinks we're all here because it's June and soon enough we'll all be off on book tours that randomly fill our summer days. You know, a last get-together until fall comes around.

Zane rubs his arms and looks around the dining room. He rented it out for this private event. He clears his throat and pulls the ring box from his pocket, nods when he sees it, and then stuffs it back.

"Why are you so nervous?" Beck asks. "This was the easiest question I ever had to ask someone."

We all erupt into a deep laugh, Simon shoving his brother-in-law and Zane flipping him off. "Sorry I didn't take shots before and run to the nearest chapel."

Beck shrugs. "Still the best decision of my life."

From the outside looking in on Beck's marriage to Calla, I thought he was crazy, considering the two of them couldn't be in a room longer than ten minutes without arguing. The phrase opposites attract is them to a tee, but then again, maybe they just needed to see how similar they were to make it work. Next month, they're having a big wedding with their friends and family.

I let out a breath, Zane's uneasy energy clinging to me.

He's about to do something life changing.

On edge or not, she's going to say yes. He's going to be happy, and they're going to get everything they want.

Tobias clears his throat when Nora, Calla, and Greer come into the room. Calla is mouthing something, and although I can't make out what it is, I have a suspicion she's letting everyone know Willa is on her way to the dining room.

My friends and I give each other space. Tobias has his phone ready to record the event.

These guys are my friends, my best friends, and we learn a lot from each other.

Well, I've learned a lot.

The biggest thing I've learned is that when it comes to my career and love life, I need to take a big risk. I'm the goody-goody who only swears quietly in his mind and has never published a book with a sex scene in it. I love routine and rules, and I'm terrified to make a change.

Yet I desperately need to. I have to do something different to have something different.

The determination to make the switch-up of a lifetime in all areas of my life—it's ready.

The light in the room turns off and the twinkling lights Zane requested shine above us. There's soft music playing in the background, with candles and flowers on every table. He didn't go all out, which is fitting for him and Willa, but it's still romantic as hell. He just wants this night to be special for her, and this room, the energy filling it, will be a night she never forgets.

I want a moment like this in my life.

No, I need a moment like this in my life.

Willa steps in, all eyes on her as she covers her mouth on a gasp and sets everything in motion.

She falls to her knees, nodding and hugging Zane, but the sign behind her catches my eye. There are two weddings at the lodge this weekend. A lot of the rich and famous come here for the big day.

One of the weddings is tonight. The reception is in another room, but it starts in an hour.

We all gather in a big circle, tossing hugs and congratulations to Zane and Willa.

Looks like I'll be attending more than one wedding myself.

I look back at the sign.

What if… I smile to myself.

What if I start this new me tonight? In an hour. Crash tonight's wedding.

I nod to myself instead of thinking it over for too long.

I'm doing it.

I'm doing something crazy.

Hell, what's the worst that could happen?

* * *

What happens when Graham crashes a wedding one night and then finds himself as the getaway driver for the bride the next day?

Find out in Write That Down!

BONUS EPILOGUE

Beck

How many books are too many books?

I place my latest release on the bookshelves in the basement with my others. A couple of years ago, Calla and I had a whole wall redone to become wall-to-wall shelving. Two of the shelves are specifically for my books and today I've successfully had to start a third shelf.

I can't believe I have fifty books. Fifty books.

It's hard not to smile when I think of how far I've come. How I thought I was successful before I met Calla, but the book I wrote that was loosely based on our story, well, it was bigger than my breakout book. I guess you could say it became my next breakout book. Either way, movie contracts on multiple books came after the release, along with book deals that I never imagined. The tour in Europe is probably one of my best memories with Calla. If we hadn't married in Vegas on a whim six years ago today, I'd have done it again in Paris.

I head down the hallway, poking my head into our office. My side of the room is a mess compared to Calla's.

Now, she not only organizes local businesses and stages homes for real estate in Wind Valley, but her company has taken over the state of Wyoming and continues to grow. Last month, she opened her first store in Colorado. She's busy nonstop, so today is a rare day that she's home and not at her office downtown.

Perks of having a full staff, I'm sure.

I jog upstairs to the back doors and find her outside unloading red brick from a wheelbarrow to place around the firepit.

"Hey, do you want help with that?" I ask. "I thought we weren't staring at this till tomorrow?"

We'd made a plan to get things done outside over the weekend. Replacing the brick was the first task on the list, but today, seeing as it's our anniversary, I had other plans for her.

"I just thought I'd get a head start, you know. Keep my mind busy." She stands and puts her hands on her hips. Her hair is cropped short at her shoulders now and the tank top and shorts show her sun-kissed skin. She's got on a pair of gardening gloves that remain dirty from all the days she's spent outside. When she moves to wipe the sweat from her forehead, which causes her shirt to rise and give me a glimpse of the skin underneath, I have to pull it together. As much as I wanted to haul her inside and into the shower to relax, I came out here with a purpose. A purpose that plays right into why she wants to keep her mind busy.

"Why don't you come inside for a minute and then I can help you finish this? I've got something I want to show you."

She playfully glares at me and crosses her arms.

"Is this like the time you wanted to show me the new pillows you chose for the couch, but then I touched it and it exploded into my face with glitter and stuffing."

I chuckle.

"No."

"What about the time that you said you needed to show me something outside and told me to put my shoes on, so I did, and they were full of shaving cream?"

I smile even wider.

"It's a real surprise."

"Mmhmm."

"Babe, I swear,"

I step for her and wrap my hands around her waist as I press my lips to hers.

"Besides, the shaving cream was payback for the glue you put in my hair gel."

She bites her bottom lip to hold back her smile and I all but growl before I kiss her again, only harder this time.

"Maybe I can show you the surprise later," I say, ready to strip her down right here, but then the surprise barks.

Her eyes light up.

"What was that?"

She peeks over my shoulder and steps for the house.

"Why don't you go inside and see."

Her smile is ear to ear and for a split second she looks at me before she goes inside to find the nine-week-old yellow lab that I bought her, I know I did my job right today. I only wish I could do more.

I follow her inside only to see that she's on the floor already with the dog climbing over her to lick her face.

"Bonding already?"

"Is he really ours?"

"Yes," I tell her. "I figured that with both our careers letting us stay home more, it was time."

"Oh, this is the best surprise ever, Beck. Thank you." She kisses his face and then picks him up to hug him. "What should we name him?"

"You pick," I say and take a seat at the table to watch my wife. I haven't seen pure joy on her face like this in months. It could make a guy cry.

"We should name him Vegas."

"Vegas. I like that."

"And then we can tell everyone that—"

She's cut off by the ringing of her phone. She sets Vegas down and grabs her phone off the counter. With wide eyes, she looks at me.

"It's them."

I stand instantly and walk to her.

"Answer it."

"Hi, this is Calla Robertson … yes … okay …" That's all she says before her free hand covers her mouth and tears quickly begin to fill her eyes.

My heart races with what's happening on the other end of the line. Is this happening? Is it finally happening?

"You're sure," Call goes on. "You're sure? … Yes, of course. Yes, yes, we will be there. Thank you. Thank you so much. Goodbye."

She slowly lowers the phone and looks at me.

"What did they say?" I ask when her mouth opens but nothing comes out.

"Someone picked us."

"Someone picked us?"

She nods. "They did and …"

"And what? What?"

"We're getting twins."

My heart hammers with joy as I lift Calla into my arms and spin her around, slowly setting her to stand and holding her tight.

"You're going to be a mom," I say softly.

"And you're going to be a dad."

Vegas barks next to us and Calla starts to laugh.

"Oh, my gosh, a puppy and two babies." Her voice grows louder and she claps. "We're going to have a puppy and two babies!"

To others, it might sound like a lot, but to me, it sounds like I'm the luckiest man in the world.

***

What happens when Graham crashes a wedding one night and then finds himself as the getaway driver for the bride the next day?

Find out in Write That Down.

MORE BOOKS BY JAMI ROGERS

For the full list of titles by Jami Rogers, please scan the QR code below.

ACKNOWLEDGMENTS

Thank you Julie, Hang Le, and Jenny for always helping me put the best book together. I've said it before and I'll say it again … I am truly lucky to have you on my team.

Dana, as always, thank you for listening to me ramble week after week about the same book until it's finished. You are more valuable to my career as a writer than you will ever know.

Grant and Brix, you are the reason I keep going. I love you!

Thank you to my family and friends for always supporting me, but most importantly, thank you to all my readers who love and share my books. You're the best!

ABOUT THE AUTHOR

My name is Jami Rogers and I write new adult contemporary and adult contemporary romance novels. I *love* love and want to share my passion for happily ever afters with the world.

I was born in Wyoming and still live in the cowboy state with my husband, daughter, and two dogs. I like to read, write, run, watch movies/TV and spend time with my family. I'm horrible at returning phone calls and prefer to text, but still struggle to hit the little blue arrow to send a message once I'm finished typing my reply. My husband does 90% of the cooking in our house. Not because I'm busy – I'm just simply a bad cook.

www.authorjamirogers.com

Want more from Jami?
Subscribe to her mailing list for exclusive bonus epilogues
and all the book news!